BEAUTY FULL

Anne Hutcheson

iUniverse LLC
Bloomington

BEAUTY FULL

This is a work of fiction. Like all works of fiction, this novel features passages wherein the reader may find himself/herself identifying with a particular character. If this should happen, please look inside your heart.

iUniverse books may be ordered through booksellers or by contacting:

iUniverse
1663 Liberty Drive
Bloomington, IN 47403
www.iuniverse.com
1-800-Authors (1-800-288-4677)

ISBN: 978-1-4917-3429-2 (sc)
ISBN: 978-1-4917-3427-8 (hc)
ISBN: 978-1-4917-3428-5 (e)

Library of Congress Control Number: 2014908176

Printed in the United States of America.

iUniverse rev. date: 04/30/2014

For Marty and Melissa:

Life is a very precious gift.

May you live yours wisely and with grace.

In spite of illness, in spite even of the archenemy sorrow, one can remain alive long past the usual date of disintegration if one is unafraid of change, insatiable in intellectual curiosity, interested in big things, and happy in small ways.

—Edith Wharton

Replenishment

Footing once secure
Now misses a step here and there,
A heartbeat now and then.
Spirit moves in swiftly,
Silently,
To quell the loss of wonder
And of hope
Paling in the waning
Light of day.

Where the majesty of mystery
And the magic of the heart
Conjoined,
There ebbs a lingering
Wish for touch,
The faintly familiar brush of lips
Softly silenced by
The loss of wonder
And of hope
Paling in the waning
Light of day.

Come hither, Spirit,
Anoint the day
And fight off the demons
Of the night.
Breathe life into my heart.
Reside in all I encounter,
For I need to reign
Once more
In the joys of wonder
And the robes of hope
Rising in the golden
Light of day.

I

Penney slowly lifted one eyelid to catch the sunbeams filling the bedroom. She lay quietly as she did a full-body stretch, her fingers and toes reaching for either end of the bed. Her husband, Jack, had risen earlier, and she could hear the clack of his computer keys from upstairs where his office was. Her other eyelid opened, and both eyes blinked as they took in the early morning, sun-dappled hues of the bedroom. Penney swung both her legs over the side of the bed and sat up. She raised her eyes to the top of the windows and watched the clouds move across the sky. A smile grew as the thought, *I am free,* also grew.

Penney had completed an extensive round of radiation treatments the day before, and in the evening she had watched an exceptional class of seniors graduate from the high school where she served as principal. These were happy thoughts, and they made Penney smile.

However, the smile slowly began to fade as Penney's mind was flooded with other memories of the past year. The heartache of others' avoidance of her over the last year tried to surface. When Penney had announced at work that she had cancer, many indicated by word or by deed that she should stop working, notably her two assistant principals, whom she had always counted previously as two very good friends. As Penney moved ahead in her role as principal, doing her job as she always had, her two assistant principals tried to rally other staff members to their cause. Their efforts were only minimally successful, but those who chose to answer the assistants' rallying cry treated Penney like an alien with a contagious disease. While few in number, there were still enough to be hurtful. Penney noticeably shivered and then shook her head to clear it of these negative thoughts, for there were many positives in the days ahead.

This particular day and its endless opportunities awaited her: prepare for the day; go to the high school; convince Jack he should meet her for lunch; maybe stop at Aimee's, her new favorite shop; go for a walk before dinner; and, oh yes, probably start brushing up on her French for the upcoming Caribbean vacation. Penney stood and stretched some more before making her way to the kitchen to grind coffee beans and brew herself an espresso. As she savored the rich, dark coffee, she called up the stairs to Jack.

"Jack, I'm up!"

"I was worried you were going to get bedsores. It's six already. How're you doing?" he replied while still audibly typing.

"Truth be told, I'm exhausted, but happy." Jack couldn't see her smile, but Penney knew he shared her happiness. "Hey, Jack, how about meeting me for lunch? You pick the place."

"Sounds good to me. I'll give you a call later this morning when I know better what my afternoon may look like. You take it easy today. Okay?"

"Yes, sir! I'm going to do the elliptical trainer for about twenty minutes and then get ready to go in to work."

"Okay!" Jack could still be heard typing away.

Penney wandered downstairs to work out, and then she moved to the master bathroom to get ready for the day. As she looked in the mirror, she sighed. Her hair was growing back. It appeared to be white-blonde in front (that's what she was calling it, and she would entertain no arguments) and dove gray in the back. It now stood about half an inch long all over her head—not long enough to unveil, but long enough to cause her scarves to slide on her head throughout the day. As for her chest, the ravages of the surgery were unpleasant to look at but easily concealed under her clothes.

Well, I had better start working my magic for the day, she thought. An hour later, magic indeed was what she had achieved. Penney looked in the mirror and assessed her work. A kicky, lime-green skirt brushed her knees, topped by a simple, white T-shirt, and the *pièce de résistance,* a boldly printed scarf complete with a swatch of lime green running through it, was tied snugly to her head. Her make-up was simple, for her eyebrows and eyelashes were growing back very slowly. A little eyebrow pencil, a soft beige eye shadow, and a tiny bit of moss-colored eyeliner made her hazel eyes pop, deemphasizing her other facial features. Penney was set for the day.

She gathered her book bag and purse and headed out the door, hollering a "Bye!" to Jack as she left. Her trip to the high school was accompanied by her favorite music, salsa. Driving alone, she could play it as loud as she liked. Loud music had always helped her think. Her thoughts drifted randomly from the high school construction project to working on the master class schedule to what she might want to shop for at Aimee's.

This would be the first day of the summer at the high school, and that meant no students. The extensive renovation project could move full steam ahead for the summer. When Penney arrived, she was amazed. She knew the construction crews had started at five o'clock this morning. There was activity all over the site. Whole walls had already been taken down, barriers had been set up, and dust roiled all over the school property. Instinctively, she had known to expect this, but taking it all in firsthand was overwhelming. *Well,* she mused, *let's hope this momentum keeps going.*

Penney found her way to the temporary offices. Here the entire guidance counseling department, the attendance clerk, her own secretaries, and her two assistant principals and their secretary had created work spaces within one large room. For herself, she had chosen to have her office set up in a service closet across the hall. All looked up when she entered, all with quizzical looks on their faces.

"Isn't this exciting?" Penney began.

"It's pretty dusty," offered the guidance secretary, Kiley.

ANNE HUTCHESON

"My allergies are already acting up," added the attendance clerk, Sondra.

Penney's two secretaries looked at one another before her personal secretary spoke. "You know, Mrs. D, it's going to be hard to work here every day if it's going to be like this. Can't they find us spaces to work downtown at the central office?"

The two assistant principals, Ted and Angie, stared at their computer screens. Penney looked their direction but got not even a flicker of their eyebrows.

"Okay. I will call Dr. Ferrari and see what I can work out."

Penney turned and walked across the hall to her office, closing the door behind her. She set her things down and then dialed Dr. Ferrari's extension number. Frank Ferrari, the school district's superintendent, she knew to be fair and open-minded. He answered on the first ring.

"Yes, Mrs. Divan." From long association, Penney knew from the timbre and tone of his voice that he was engaged with his computer screen.

"Frank, we need to talk about working conditions for the summer. The dust is incredible. There are huge gaping holes, so if it rains, that dust will turn to mud. I don't have to tell you what needs to be done by my staff over the summer. I do know they won't compromise their efforts. I am wondering if they can't do some of their work off-site."

"So, they are already complaining to you. The answer is yes, but not downtown. You work it out. They can work from their homes if they want. Just tell me when they won't be at the high school."

"Thank you. I assume you are okay with them dressing down for these conditions."

"Sure. Do what you have to do. Nice graduation speech last night. It always amazes me that your students really don't hold back showing how much they like you. I've said this before, but it still astounds me when your graduates hug you onstage. You are the only principal I have ever seen students hug in all my years of experience. Okay. Gotta go. Talk to you soon."

"Bye, Frank. And thank you."

Penney walked briskly back across the hall. She explained how they would proceed. Sondra continued on about her allergies. Penney fingered her scarf as she gave tentative permission to Sondra to work from home when Sondra thought her health might be jeopardized. The others seemed to be copacetic with what Frank had offered.

Sean, Penney's principal intern, arrived as Penney was finishing. Penney asked Kiley and her two assistant principals to join Sean and herself for course scheduling in one of the open classrooms. However, the assistant principals never did join them.

As Penney, Sean, and Kiley sat down and got to work, Kiley did comment after a few minutes into the scheduling, "Gosh! I wonder what is keeping Ted and Angie."

Sean raised an eyebrow but kept focused on his computer screen.

"They have quite a bit to do with discipline yet for the school year. The state department needs that data by the end of the month. And remember, Ted is leaving to join another school district soon, so he probably wants to help Angie all that he can right now," Penney replied. She too did not look up from her computer.

Penney, Sean, and Kiley worked for a few hours on the master schedule. As the three of them finished up for the morning, each with assignments to address regarding the schedule before they met the next morning, Penney briefly pondered why the assistant principals were so obstinate. She knew they had not agreed with her when she chose to keep working in spite of her cancer diagnosis. Yet, it was her decision alone to make. In addition, from Penney's perspective, the real bottom line was that if Ted and Angie did indeed want to be principals of their own schools one day, they had to know that a finely tuned and well-orchestrated master schedule under their direction was essential for any school to operate efficiently. Tweaking the schedule as the school year progressed was costly in terms of general operations and especially in maintaining strong leadership. Distancing oneself from the process was deadly in Penney's opinion. Overseeing the evolution of the master schedule now meant the principal could perform his or her real role throughout the remainder of the year, that of instructional leadership. Frank certainly understood this, and Penney was quite certain this was why she had virtually full command of the high school. She did not know too many principals who had her unfettered power and authority.

True, Ted would be leaving soon. Angie, on the other hand, Penney couldn't figure out. There came that heartache from vanishing friends, for Ted and Angie had been good friends, and their lost support had been devastating initially. Cancer, she had learned, was very poorly understood by far too many people. Penney's own cancer, a form of triple-negative cancer called metaplastic carcinoma, was aggressive and rare. Even her doctors knew little about it; a few of them knew nothing about it. That did not keep the "resident experts" from letting her know what she should and should not be doing. Penney let out a deep sigh, closed her eyes, and visualized balloons carrying off all her negative thoughts and feelings. Knowing full well such thoughts would further zap her energies, Penney had learned how to recapture her focus.

Penney called Jack, and together they arranged to meet for lunch at their favorite restaurant with a deck so they could eat outside. Having packed her own paperwork back up, Penney crossed the hall to let everyone know that they too could take their laptops with them to work from their homes for the remainder of the afternoon. After lunch, Penney stopped by Aimee's for a peek at the new things arriving for the summer. She left with a fun red sundress after trying on several things.

Arriving home, Jack was ready to go for a walk. They changed into walking shoes and walked about three miles through their neighborhood. It was somewhat hilly, and consequently what appeared to be a casual stroll was actually a challenging hike.

While Jack grilled fish on the barbecue for their dinner, Penney sat down with a French CD and accompanying text to review some basic French terms. Penney and Jack would be vacationing on the island of Guadeloupe at the end of the month. Penney had read that only French was spoken on this Caribbean island.

As with everything, Penney wanted to be prepared. She took the Guadeloupe guidebook to bed with her that night and dreamt of sapphire-blue waters, waving fields of cane, amethyst sunsets, and beckoning beaches.

II

Penney's days were now filled with an old, familiar urgency. The master class schedule had to be in pretty good shape before she left on vacation. It was not unlike any other summer, but Penney knew she needed this common routine at this time in her life more than ever. Free of the cancer that had plagued her for the previous year, she relished working relatively unencumbered on a project that she vanquished every summer. True, when she left the high school each day, Penney trooped off to the acupuncturist, the lymphedema specialist, the masseuse, or the spiritual healer. These were the people who made her feel safe in a world she had had to learn to tread with care. These were the people who understood she needed an ear to listen and a smile to ease her discomforts when they arose. These were the people who cared for her and befriended her. These were the people Penney desperately needed.

Penney walked determinedly to the room where the master class schedule would begin to take shape. Sean, Kiley, and Penney would work on the master schedule diligently for the next two weeks. They would let the computer do its thing, but the diversity of the course selections would prove to be the nemesis of the new computer scheduling program. At the end of each day, Penney would reload the scheduling boards lining the walls of the classroom where they worked. She would survey these boards before she left each day, committing each teacher's proposed class schedule to memory. Penney's dreams were filled with this data, and she awakened each day with ideas to rearrange particular class times. Sean often e-mailed her with his own thoughts late at night. Their early-morning e-mail exchanges were lively, giving them direction for this and every day. Kiley entered their requests into the computer program each morning. Sometimes their requests were brilliant; other times, not so much.

As the course scheduling and state reports seemed to be moving along, Ted left one day near the end of the month. With no details offered regarding his impending departure, Penney knew it was coming but did not know when. He now appeared in Penney's office carrying an antique box Penney had long admired in his office.

"So, would you like this? I don't plan on taking it with me." Ted made no eye contact with Penney and pointedly stared at a space over his shoulder while juggling the beautifully carved but cumbersome box.

"Sure. Happy to take it off your hands. Just set it on the table. And good luck, Ted." Penney could feel her own long-dormant feelings of friendship trying to surface.

Though Penney looked directly at him, Ted continued to be diverted by something in the distance. He placed the box on the table, nodded at nothing in particular, and walked out of Penney's life.

Formerly, Penney would have been distressed, but she had lost Ted as a friend the day she told him she had cancer. Thinking he would take over managing the high school, Ted was appalled when Penney informed him she would continue to work. He had been a source of pain and of negativity for much of the past year. There was no longer any place for anything other than the positive anymore in Penney's life. *Odd that he would leave me a gift.* Penney closed her eyes and listened to her breathing until her cell phone started ringing. The construction supervisor needed to speak with her about limiting access to the building. *Back to the real world, Penney.*

She smiled and trundled out to the construction supervisor's trailer. There, together the two of them looked at options for the summer staff to move safely in and out of the building. Returning to her office, Penney carefully wended her way around construction workers, vehicles, equipment, and supplies. *This activity is exciting,* Penney thought, *despite all the inconveniences.*

She ran into Angie on her way back to the office. "Hey, Angie! We're missing you at our scheduling sessions."

"Oh, well, I just figured you can do it yourself." Angie was fidgeting like a trapped animal.

Frank had repeatedly told Penney not to make a big deal out of Angie's dismissals. Consequently, Penney pushed her gut-level response away to cheerfully say, "Should you need any help with the state reports, just let me know."

Penney smiled at Angie, who stared back vacantly in return, still shuffling from one foot to the other. As Penney moved on to her office, she waved to Angie. Angie remained standing in the same spot, just looking at Penney.

Briefly debating the wisdom of her next action, since she did not want it to sound like she was complaining, Penney dialed Frank's extension. He picked up right away, so Penney moved right on to what was clouding her mind.

"Frank, I just had two of the strangest encounters." She told Frank about the gift delivery, to which he responded with a deep laugh. Penney then described her encounter with Angie.

"Penney, Angie has been to see me. She's worried you are going to yell at her. I did ask if you had any reason to yell at her, but she could not think of any reason."

"Frank, Frank, Frank, you know perfectly well..."

Frank interrupted to say, "Penney, I do know. But it is you I am worried about. Ignore her. It will be better now that Ted is gone. You still have her evaluation to do. Address your concerns there. Now, how is that master schedule coming?"

"It will be a work of art, I can assure you."

With that, they concluded their conversation. Penney sat down at her desk and wrote the most difficult evaluation she had ever written in her career. Difficult, yes, but necessary. Penney e-mailed Angie with a time for going over the evaluation the very next day. Then she moved on to meet with Sean and Kiley to put several issues to rest regarding the master schedule. At the end of the day, all three of them agreed the schedule was really coming along nicely. Classes were filling, and the numbers in each class were beginning to balance.

The next morning, Angie sat across from Penney and carefully read her evaluation. Angie glanced up when she was done, reached for the pen on the table, signed the evaluation, and stood up.

"Do you have any questions? Or perhaps concerns I could address?" Penney inquired, somewhat disconcerted by Angie's abruptness again.

Angie shook her head no. Her eyes were starting to well up with tears as she turned and left Penney's office.

Penney signed the evaluation herself. She affirmed that the assessment was fair. Angie's strengths had been elaborated, as had her failures to meet a few of Penney's expectations, notably following through on specific requests and not always communicating in a professional manner. Penney surprised herself by concluding that her relationship with Angie could only improve from this point forward. Penney made copies of the evaluation, put them in the interoffice mail, and then proceeded with the rest of her day.

Before she left the high school that afternoon, Penney did pull up the state reports to see how they were coming. The attendance and guidance reports were almost finished. The discipline report was not even half complete. It appeared Angie was going to have to talk to her, whether Angie wanted to or not. When Penney put in a call to Frank to share her concern, he initially exploded.

"What? You and I both have to sign off on all those reports!" Following a pregnant pause, he added, "I did read Angie's evaluation a little bit ago. It was very well written. So, Mrs. Divan, I am sure you will pull everything together, and I have nothing to worry about.

My brother and I are taking my mother out to dinner, so I'm out of here. Talk to you tomorrow."

For Penney's part, she knew she had much to do in a short amount of time. Those Caribbean beaches were looking better and better.

Intruding on these delicious thoughts, however, was an all-too-familiar nag. There was that latent pain again, a pain lingering since the surgery nearly a year ago. It popped up every once in a while, like the heartache did from time to time. Stress seemed to exacerbate this pain and the heartache. Penney had mentioned the pain to Nell, her lymphedema specialist, and both the pain and heartache to Karishma, her acupuncturist. They had both recommended Reiki to supplement their treatments. It was worth a try, Penney had decided. That surgery site just did not seem to want to give up the ghost. A little self-massage did help, and Penney was back to scheduling for a few hours before bed. A Reiki session awaited her later in the week.

As Penney awoke the next morning, she knew she would have to begin her work day very carefully. Dressing in her power mode was a little dicey with all the construction. Nonetheless, she felt like she did have to make a striking statement with Angie, and her appearance was part of the message. Penney pushed herself on the elliptical trainer this morning. She gave studious attention to planning her outfit. A muted brown pantsuit with dress shirt and pumps was topped off with a dark brown scarf. She drove thoughtfully in to work and immediately asked her personal secretary to send Angie to her office. Laying her other things aside, Penney opened her laptop at the conference table to the state discipline report.

Angie arrived dressed in Bermudas, a tank top, and flip-flops. It crossed Penney's mind that she had been meaning to talk to Angie about dressing more professionally. That conversation, however, would just have to wait.

Penney asked Angie to have a seat and began, "Good morning. I have been looking over all of the state reports, and I am concerned that the discipline report you have been working on still needs a lot of work. Would you like some help? Are there some questions I might be able to answer? It is due for me to look over on Monday."

Angie looked at Penney placidly and said quietly, "I was just figuring you would have changes anyway and would be finishing it off."

"Discipline is your primary responsibility in regard to the students. This report is a review of your disciplinary procedures for the past school year. You handle student discipline well. I am trusting you will complete this report well and on time. Should questions arise, I am happy to sit down with you and discuss them. I will again emphasize that this report is due in my office Monday. Now, we had both better get to work. If you would like to help with the scheduling, your input would be appreciated."

Penney stood, indicating the meeting was over. She walked over to the door and held it open for Angie. Lumbering out of her chair, Angie gave Penney a bothered look and walked slowly across the hall.

Ay-yi-yi! Penney massaged her temples. *It's going to be a very long summer.* She sat down to make a list prioritizing what needed to be pretty much done before she left on vacation and what could wait until she returned. This pointed her right back to the master schedule. She changed into a pair of comfortable shoes, put her suit jacket aside, and rolled up her sleeves. Penney was shooting for seventy-five percent of the master schedule to be done today. At the end of the day, Sean, Kiley, and Penney were very close to that goal. Penney also took a look at the disciplinary report and happily discovered that progress had been made.

Arriving home, Penney was eager to hike the neighborhood with Jack. The pace was rapid and left the two of them breathless. During the walk, Penney shared her day with Jack, who shook his head as he had so many times over the Angie trials. He called it insubordination; Penney called it immaturity.

Jack had another concern he wanted to share. "You know, Penney, you have been driving yourself pretty hard since graduation. You probably need to slow down just a little, or I am afraid you're going to crash and burn. How about it, Penney?"

"Aw, Jack, I'm fine. I do sit quietly at some point during the day. All my late-afternoon appointments make it essential for me to stop and relax. And I am going to give Reiki a shot to see if it ultimately will help me sleep. There's Guadeloupe coming up too."

"I am going to insist that on Guadeloupe you make a good effort to just chill. You don't have to be on the go every minute. This Reiki thing sounds like hocus-pocus to me, but so does some of your other stuff, and they work for you. So…I'll wait and see. Bottom line, Penney, I think you need more rest." Jack was looking directly at Penney, and he had taken her hands in his as he talked.

Penney withdrew her hands, which she now placed on her hips. "Jack, I'm fine. Yes, I do need to rest better, and all my hocus-pocus does help. Now, I am off to see how to translate hocus-pocus into French." Penney marched off in the direction of her study.

Jack repaired to the kitchen to start dinner, which was therapeutic for him, while Penney grappled with French vocabulary, which was therapeutic for her. All she came up with for hocus-pocus was *magie,* which really meant magic. *Well, you know,* Penney thought, *I am getting something out of the magic.* Penney's dreams that night were once again filled with moving classes around on the scheduling boards, but on this night the class names were all magically in French.

III

The master class schedule and state reports were shaping up well as the end of the week approached. Penney's persistence was paying off. As she drove to meet with the Reiki master, Penney was feeling sure of herself and pleased with her staff. The majority of them were actually having fun with the relaxed dress code and with the freedom to pick where they did their work.

Arriving at the yoga center, Penney parked her car in the shade and walked along the carefully landscaped walkway. Quiet was requested on a sign as she entered the door. The next sign asked that shoes be removed, which she did. As she entered the office, Penney's eyes were drawn to the top of the cathedral ceilings and then back to the simple but tasteful furnishings and wall hangings. Soft candlelight added to the serene setting. As she waited for the Reiki master, Penney took in the gentle flowing of the water in the fountain, the various deities displayed around the room, and the tranquil ambience created by the calming influences surrounding her. Not the least of these effects was the choice of colors used in the room: a soft, petal pink; a dusky, cloudy lavender; the bluish gray of the sky on a hazy summer's eve. Penney felt a peacefulness settling around her.

A slight sense of movement redirected Penney's attention. Cree entered the doorway, not with her physical presence so much as by her compelling aura. There was a soft golden cast surrounding her. She was, in fact, petite. Her caramel-highlighted hair was pulled back in a ponytail, and her cocoa-colored eyes flashed brightly above her welcoming smile.

"Hi, I'm Cree. You are Penney, correct?" The radiance of the glow which enshrouded Cree could not be mistaken.

"Yes, I am. I am pleased to meet you," replied Penney as she stood to shake Cree's hand.

"I just thought we would talk about Reiki for a few moments. Then I can answer any questions you may have. So, please, have a seat."

As they both settled into their seats, Cree began, "Reiki is a spiritual healing process. Using very gentle touch, I am going to lead your body in a healing process, emotionally, mentally, physically, and spiritually. To do this, I am going to channel our energies. In conjunction with your other forms of healing, I will enhance your overall health, vitality, and well-being. Understand that Reiki does not treat disease, but rather it helps to restore balance. What questions do you have that I might try to answer?"

"I have looked into Reiki as a healing source with my acupuncturist, my lymphedema specialist, and my spiritual healer. We are all interested in improving my sleep primarily, at least to begin with."

"I hope to help you reduce stress and aid you in achieving relaxation in order to bring the balance I have mentioned. You should find your sleep enhanced in no time. So, shall we begin?"

Penney followed Cree to a room across the hall. The room was welcoming and filled with the tender tones of chimes coming from the CD player. Cree instructed Penney to lie on the table on her back with her spine straight. Cree gently placed a lavender-filled eye pillow over Penney's eyes. And they began.

Starting with the feet, Cree tenderly clasped both her hands around each of Penney's feet. Penney could feel her whole body relax as energy flowed from Cree's hands to Penney's feet and on through her entire body. Ever so slowly, Cree worked her way over Penney's body, moving next to Penney's ankles, legs, kneecaps, and thighs, resting her palms in each position for several minutes before moving on to the next. From Penney's thighs, Cree moved her hands round to Penney's lower back and then to the sides of her hips. By the time Cree moved her palms to form a V-shape above the pelvic area, the energy being channeled between Cree and Penney was electrifying. Not a word was spoken, but the energies exchanged between the two women were speaking mightily. As Cree positioned her hands one above the other, one on the upper abdomen and the other on the lower abdomen, her breaths were deep and long as she too took in the energy emanating from Penney's body. Moving further, Cree placed her right hand over the area under Penney's ribs on the right side of her body, and she placed her left hand on the upper left side of her abdomen. Once arriving at the lungs, Cree lightly rested her palms in line with them. By this point, Penney could breathe in only the positive energy her body so badly craved. Her breath was now calmer, her state of mind relaxed. Penney was quiet and peaceful. Cree next placed both her hands over Penney's heart. As Cree moved her palms around Penney's neck and around her shoulders, she could feel some tension in Penney's neck, which she now lingered over. With a downward and forward movement, Cree slid her palms from Penney's ears to her jawline. Cupping Penney's jaw between her palms, she supported Penney's head. The intense energy buildup in the room was extraordinary at this point. Cree carefully moved both her hands backward so that her palms rested above Penney's ears. As Cree made this movement, she let the tips of her fingers brush away any lingering stress from Penney's forehead. This indeed left Penney in a euphoric state. Cree ever so gently removed the eye pillow from Penney's eyes and slowly slid her palms over the top of Penney's head so that they came to rest over her eyes. Penney and Cree could both feel the tingling heat within the palms of Cree's hands. Penney's mind and body were both totally relaxed as Cree placed her hands at the top of Penney's head, arranging her hands slightly to the back of Penney's head. Her palms softly touched Penney's head. Calm fell over the room like new-fallen snow. Cree left the room after quietly telling Penney to take several deep breaths before she got up from the table.

Penney slowly opened her eyes and took in the lingering yellow light of the setting sun filtering through the room's one window. Her heart, her mind, and her body were still. Her spirit, however, engulfed the space around her. In this moment, she was not only at peace, but also attuned to every fiber in her being. She could still feel the sensation of Cree's touch up and down her body.

Penney dawdled as she got up from the table. A smile was beginning to form as she thought about what Jack would make of all this. She made her way across the hall to the office, feeling lighter than air itself. Penney and Cree shared their experiences of the past seventy-five minutes. Penney could not say how wonderful it was enough times. Cree explained how she could see her hands melt into Penney's body several times, Penney's body being keenly receptive to the energy being channeled during the session. The two hugged, and Penney floated out to her car.

Jack, of course, wanted to know immediately upon her arrival home what took place at one of these Reiki sessions.

"Jack, energy just flowed between Cree and me. It was one of the most intense, while at the same time most relaxing, experiences I have ever had. You should try it."

"If it's good for you, Penney, then I will take part vicariously through you." Jack winked at Penney.

"Jack…" Penney could see him struggling to stifle his smirk.

"Seriously, if it works for you, then it's good for me. Let's go out for dinner."

With that, Jack knew all he needed to know about Reiki. It surely sounded like hocus-pocus, but if it made Penney feel better, he was good with it. *Strange, though, that she didn't even get a massage out of it!* Penney slept soundly through the night.

The next morning, she felt calmly energized. Her meditation, workout, and scheduling at work she did with a deliberate sense of how grateful she was to be doing these activities. Sensing a lack of calm among her summer staff, who were working on top of one another, after all, Penney called them together to ask them to prepare for a tour of the construction project. There were treasures out there waiting to be viewed, and she wanted to share them with the people who worked literally within the project. After making sure that each of them wore closed-toe shoes and a hard hat, she led her staff out to the path she herself used to inspect the project. Penney could already feel and hear them lightening up a little. Their comments suggested a congenial curiosity and heady anticipation of what they might see. As they approached the new gymnasium, the group of men working on the roof looked at one another. Getting closer, one of the men stepped near the edge to address Penney, who was slowly leading her group in single file over, under, around, and through debris, materials, and equipment.

"Hey! You can't cross the barriers! This is an active work site!"

Penney stopped her staff with one hand held up. Then she placed both hands on her hips and looked up. The guy loomed large up there—probably pushing forty, but with muscles bulging and sweat causing his t-shirt to cling to his chest where a little paunch protruded beneath.

"You know you have seen me walk this route every day now for over a week. I have informed my group here that there may be no wandering. So, hey yourself! I might point out that this is my building."

"She's got you on that last point, Brady." A chuckle rippled through the workers on the roof.

"Yep, she does. Okay, ma'am, go on through, but please be careful."

"Thanks! And in the future, Brady, my name is Penney."

Penney's staff continued on to the partition that allowed access to the gymnasium. She slid the temporary closure aside, and each member of her staff entered, catching their breaths as they gazed up and down taking in the shimmering wood floor, the vast number of seats, and the state–of–the–art scoreboard fixedly peering over the entire space.

Sean was the first to speak. "Mrs. D, this is beyond my wildest imagination. All I can say is wow! And wow! And wow some more!"

Turning slowly around, Penney's personal secretary added, "This is amazing, Mrs. D."

All, in turn, marveled at the sheer luxury surrounding them.

"I know this is hard on all of you, but I am very insistent that each stage of this project turn out as nice as this. I try to keep looking ahead and to keep my eye on the prize."

The group stayed in the gym another twenty minutes taking in every nook and cranny. Penney and Sean even took turns taking virtual shots at one of the baskets to the cheers of the others. They journeyed on around the project, but the nearly completed gymnasium lingered in their minds' eyes.

Once they were back in the office, work took on a new dimension with everyone much more effortlessly involved with their tasks. Even Angie appeared to be intently engaged with her computer screen, though quieter than the others. Friday ended on a positive note, and the weekend began.

The weekend was rather uneventful for Penney. Both she and Jack were enjoying these days, when all seemed as it had been again. They hiked a little each day, prepared meals together, and slept a lot. Penney worked on her French off and on.

First thing Monday morning found Penney at her desk at home checking the state reports. Guidance, attendance, and discipline were all complete. Penney leaned back from her desk, relieved. She would meet with each of the persons responsible for each report today. This included Angie. Penney was not overly excited about meeting with her. Penney knew to expect little, if any, effect. It seemed to Penney that a person ought to get excited about a job well done in a positive way. Well, she would do that for every one of them! Dressing in bright colors, Penney was hoping she could expect a little sparkle in her day.

The state report reviews went well, even Angie's, which almost yielded a smile from her. They all knew from past experience that the reports would be returned with requested revisions noted. However,

Penney felt pretty good about them and reported their completion to Frank.

"Good morning, Frank!"

"And good morning to you, Mrs. Divan! What can I do for you?"

"I am forwarding the state reports to you. They appear to be in order, but as you know, the education gurus can pick out some pretty obscure things for us to take a second look at."

"Let's hope there aren't too many."

Penney was finding his uncharacteristic affability a little disconcerting. But then maybe Frank too had had a Reiki session! Following this fleeting thought, Penney had to stifle a giggle that wanted to erupt from her throat.

"You know, Penney, there may be a position coming open here at central office in elementary curriculum. How do you think this might fit Angie's skills?"

"Hmmm…you know, she is so young and will be in education for a very long time. This would be an opportunity for her to extend her skill set and to get a feel for another level. She has talked about pursuing her superintendent's papers. This could give her a whole new perspective."

"Fine! If the opening comes up, I think I will talk to her about it. That might leave you without an assistant principal for a while."

"Advancing a young person's career comes first. How many applications do we have?"

"Quite a few, actually, since the recent posting, plus a few that came in prior to the posting. A couple you will recognize from earlier openings."

"Just as soon as HR is done with them, please send them my way so we can start setting up interviews."

"You got it! Now, on to the master schedule. How's it coming along?"

"Slow but steady. It's shaping up nicely. I am hoping I can send it along to the guidance counselors by mid-July when they are in to work on their contracted days."

"Sounds good. If I don't talk to you before your vacation, have a relaxing good time. How's your French?"

"It too is coming along. And thanks, Frank!"

"See ya!"

Penney thought to herself, *Shrewd man, that Frank!* This potential opening actually could be a very good move for Angie, and it would undeniably cause less negativity in Penney's own life. Hanging up the phone, Penney did laugh out loud as her thoughts flitted to the image of Frank on the Reiki table. She pulled herself together and went in search of Sean and Kiley. Together, the three of them worked on the master schedule until well into the afternoon.

Penney's week was rounded out with visits to her spiritual healer, her primary care physician for a routine checkup and blood work, and the spa, of course, to get her nails done for the trip. She took Friday as a personal day to finish preparing for the vacation and to assure everyone she was resting.

From the airplane, Penney observed white, puffy clouds as she looked down from a baby-blue sky onto indigo-colored waters. Penney took a breath and then took in the view again. *A real Caribbean vacation—sun, sand, sleep, and French.* Immediately upon setting foot on the tarmac, Penney's brain was bombarded with French. She got herself and Jack through baggage claim, the car rental agency, and asking for directions to the resort.

"Penney, I have to say that was amazing! You actually learned all that from a book and a CD?"

"Well, my high school and college French have stuck with me, but I can also say I amazed myself!"

They both laughed. Their attention was drawn to the roadside where the sea shimmered in the distance, hosting surfers riding the waves as a backdrop to small shops and restaurants dotting the road. Pulling up to their resort, they found a lush garden setting with iguanas freely roaming the grounds. Penney got them through registration successfully and into their room. They tossed their things onto the bed and quickly returned to the road in search of a late lunch. Codfish fritters, sea bream, and bananas flambé turned out to be a delicious introduction to the island's cuisine.

Next, Penney and Jack began their exploration of the island. Their days would be filled with fine food, French wines, and leisurely drives to markets offering jewelry made from seeds, pungent bags of spices, and brilliant madras textiles. They would tour lovely, old creole homes, historical museums and sites, rum distilleries, the aquarium (which included a turtle rescue station, much to Penney's delight), the exquisite botanical gardens, and the zoo, which would offer Penney and Jack a new challenge.

After purchasing their tickets to the animal park, Penney carefully studied the informational brochure. *A canopy,* she thought, *and why not?* They made their way to the refreshment area, where hummingbirds perched, ready for their share of the juice offered gratis. Penney and Jack thrilled in the unreserved familiarity with which the hummingbirds helped themselves to their and everyone else's drinks. Moving on, Penney spied the entrance to the canopy. No one was waiting, so she quickly walked up to outfit herself in the harness and gear attaching her to the overhead pulley. Jack followed suit.

"Penney, are you sure this is something you want to do?" Jack was sounding a little tremulous. Penney knew that he was not liking the potential for testing his fear of heights.

"Jack, come on. If not now, then when? Let's go for it!"

The path beckoned ahead—two two-by-fours suspended over what appeared to be a luxuriant, tropical forest. There were ropes to hang on to along the sides, and, after all, they were attached overhead. They began the march, albeit slowly. For the first few minutes, they walked directly above the tree line. Lush, green tropical rainforest surrounded them. It was not unlike being suspended in a tropical greenhouse. Flora and fauna indigenous to the West Indies brushed their feet, their heads, and their shoulders. Very quickly, they peered down for overhead views of raccoons, iguanas, tortoises, and gaily festooned parrots. The sleek, black panthers stopped Penney and Jack in their tracks as the panthers moved their muscular bodies with an ease and grace reminiscent of ballet dancers. It was breathtaking! And then they came to a bend in the path.

The turn had only one two-by-four going around a tree. It was going to require unhooking from the overhead pulley to step around the tree carefully, and then each of them individually reattaching to the line overhead.

"Penney, this is a problem."

"Jack, since I go first, I'll help you. For heaven's sake, please don't look down!" Penney smiled with all her might while thinking *Oops! This was not in the brochure.*

Penney made the maneuver with deliberate care. She smiled encouragingly at Jack and held out her hand.

"Penney, we are not doing this canopy thing again. It is too unnerving." Jack undid his harness attachment from the pulley overhead and cautiously wrapped himself around the tree before placing one foot carefully on the other side of the tree. Penney bent in to replace his attachment as his other foot edged around the tree.

Whew! "Okay! We did it!" Penney was relieved but felt a little triumphant too. "Don't you feel a little like Tarzan up here?" she asked playfully.

"Never again, Penney! This is just too scary!" Jack was sweating profusely and, Penney could see, noticeably trembling.

"Perhaps not as scary as cancer," Penney said contemplatively. "We did it! We're doing it! What a way to view the animals, Jack! Let's enjoy the rest of our adventure!"

"Okay! Okay! But can we move slowly, please? And I am not doing this again."

The animals continued to amaze them from their perch above. The jaguars were quite active when Penney and Jack passed overhead to watch the big cats tease one another as if they were kittens. Still, Jack was mighty glad when he could climb out of his harness and join Penney for a close-up view of the orchid garden and the impressive collection of insects, standing on his own two feet on firm ground. Both laughed about it afterward as they dined on lobster and conch and enjoyed the live bands playing beguine and zouk, popular rhythms of the island. Following the lead of their fellow diners, Penney and Jack also found these rhythms very danceable.

The next day, while Penney was watching people pass by their sidewalk table, she mentioned to Jack that the majority of the women on the island, including the Europeans, wore their hair pretty short.

"You know, Penney, I think it may be time to unveil your own short hair. I kinda like it. It suits you, sorta sassy and fun."

"Let me think about it," Penney answered as she continued her observations. Penney carefully assessed several more women as they passed the table. There were pixie haircuts and closely cropped haircuts. Penney found herself drawn to the women's facial features, for the short hair served as a frame for coquettish makeup, emphasizing eyes and cheekbones. Maybe, just maybe, she too could pull off this look.

That evening, Penney left her scarf behind when they went to dinner. She realized she was just another woman on the island who wore her hair very short. It was a big moment and a liberating one. Penney had shorn one more reminder of her cancer.

Their remaining days were filled with hiking, sunbathing, and enjoying the sultry, sensuous evenings with dining and dancing. Penney stood on the beach their last evening drinking in the sights, sounds, and smells of this Caribbean island. Jack stood beside her as he watched her hair shimmer in the glow of the moonlight over the water and her whole being bask in the glow of slowly returning good health.

It had been a good week and a very good trip. There had been very little time for e-mails. Those that did arrive announced Angie's move to central office, as well as a nearly complete master schedule. Penney spent little time poring over them, however, because speaking French nearly round the clock was proving taxing to her brain and her energy. In the end, though, Penney could take pride in speaking French with somewhat of a flair by the close of the week.

IV

When Penney returned to work, her hair did not cause much of a stir. Her two secretaries pronounced it cute, and life at the high school moved on. The master course schedule Sean, Kiley, and Penney tweaked here and there, but Penney determined it was ready to turn over to the guidance counselors. Penney did a walk through the construction site with the construction supervisor and marveled at the progress made in one short week. Old classrooms were being transformed into a guidance counseling suite, and Penney could see this space taking shape with walls and offices now roughed out. She eagerly looked forward to showing the new suite to the guidance counselors. Angie's absence was not mentioned. The tone in the office was light, and laughter came readily as all attended to their duties.

The end of that first day back at work also brought a follow-up oncology visit. Penney was actually looking forward to the visit as she knew a temporary replacement for her previous oncologist, Dr. Sriram, should be in place. She was really hoping for someone who would answer her questions directly. Like a breath of fresh air, Dr. Bradley entered the exam room—tall, and taller yet with her stiletto heels. Her statuesque figure was complemented by long, dark hair complete with peek-a-boo bangs and a playful twinkle in her blue eyes.

Grabbing Penney's right hand with both of her hands, Dr. Bradley launched right into her introduction. "Good afternoon, Penney! I'm Dr. Bradley. I'll be filling in for the summer. I have to tell you up front that breast cancer has not been my focus, but I am somewhat familiar with your type of cancer, which is a rather daunting type of triple-negative cancer. I hope you brought questions. I will do my best to answer any you may have."

"I am happy to meet you! Yes, I do have quite a few questions." Penney took in Dr. Bradley's genuine eagerness to help her, but with a bit of expectant reticence.

"Let's have a look at you first and then get right to your questions."

As the exam began, the questions actually were triggered from the beginning.

"As you can see, the whole irradiated area is pretty raw and can be quite itchy," Penney pointed out.

"What topical cream are you using on this?" Dr. Bradley inquired as she looked over the area very carefully.

"Aloe."

"I know it may be a pain—and please, no pun intended—but I would like you to use the aloe several times a day on this affected area. Also, I notice you're wincing a little as I work around and above the incision area, as well as the area treated with radiation."

"Yes, it is very, very tender."

"When do you see your radiation oncologist?"

"Tomorrow."

"Be sure you bring these issues up with him as well. Now, what else can I answer for you?"

Penney explained her sleep troubles, how she was often waking up at crazy, wee hours of the morning with racing heart and trembling limbs. She confirmed that the ridges and cloudiness in her nails were due to chemotherapy and would just have to continue to grow out. *Sigh...* She mentioned her ongoing congestion, intermittent headaches, vaginal dryness, and dry mouth. Dr. Bradley gave her several ideas to try using natural remedies. Penney moved on with her questions, working up to a couple of big ones.

"I have been told I should hold off coloring my hair. I can't seem to get a reason, although I have explored the topic."

"I know the nurses are usually adamant about not using hair color and nail color. There is really no reason why you can't. Be crazy with color if you like."

Penney now smiled broadly, but briefly. Her final question was huge for her.

"Like all cancer patients, I want to know my likelihood for recurrence." Her tone was nakedly plaintive.

"I spent a long time yesterday going through your file. I hope you understand that you have survived one mean, aggressive cancer. I would say you have a five to six percent chance for a recurrence. I'll order scans for you for later this summer, after the radiation site has calmed down a little, so that we can get an updated look at you."

Penney was beaming. This was so much better than what she had been expecting. She wanted to stand up and dance.

Dr. Bradley smiled back at her. "So, Penney, in August we'll do scans, probably a mammogram too, and maybe an MRI to take a closer look at your headaches. I'll see you after I get the results. Enjoy your summer!"

They shook hands. Penney left happy, happy, happy. She had had an actual conversation with this oncologist and had learned that she did have hope.

She returned to the hospital the next day to meet with Dr. Ryden, her dogmatic radiation oncologist. He listened to what she had learned when meeting with Dr. Bradley and responded with a "Humpph!" He thought it was time she looked at metaplastic carcinoma a little more closely. He took Penney to his office, where together they looked at recent abstracts related to metaplastic carcinoma. He translated the technical information, but the gist was that she shouldn't get her hopes up. Her optimism from the day before prevailed, though, and she left Dr. Ryden's office thinking, *I just want to be happy for now.* After all the grim forecasts and dire predictions from all the doctors over most of the last year, Penney had survived and wanted only life to look forward to. When Jack returned from a business trip later that week, he reveled in Penney's good news and underscored that she most certainly was to be happy. Their longtime friends, Hannah and Harry, also confirmed this right to happiness during their monthly phone call. Penney and Hannah shared the bond of survivorship with their cancer experiences. "Life forward" was their motto.

The next several weeks were busy at work with parent meetings, construction meetings, administrators' meetings, and preparing materials for the staff's return to work in late August. Many staff members tentatively sought Penney out for lunches or for drinks after work. Penney knew the majority of them were happy to see her looking healthy again, and they wanted to share her new health with her. A few of them, however, had been among Ted and Angie's followers. These latter exchanges she engaged with a polite reserve when she did agree to meet. Penney wanted to dodge the heartache of mistrust as best she could. She desperately still missed her old familiarity and frank openness with all of her staff, but the past year had taught her to be cautious. Penney still had nightmares where she walked the halls of the high school with the eyes of that small group of staff she had grown to mistrust following her until she passed their classroom doors. When she continued down the hallways, Penney could hear their classroom doors and their hearts click shut. She simply could not endure the thoughts those images conjured up.

For the most part, Penney's after-work schedule was pretty busy with a series of alternative medicine therapies, all slowly leading her back to good health. Many seemed befuddled that she continued to do all this. Their query almost always went something like this: "You're still doing all that? I thought you were finished with everything." *Isn't it odd,* Penney could not help thinking, *that cardiac patients get exercise and lifestyle instruction, and injury patients get physical and occupational therapy—but cancer patients, on the other hand, are expected to exit treatment and slog through years of recovery and/or repeated onslaughts of cancer with little, if any, guidance?* She preferred not to think about what that might mean for their long-term prognosis.

Penney's own research now focused on after-cancer treatments. Her exercise regimen was beefed up to rebuild her strength. Her diet she increasingly modified, focusing on fresh, cruciferous vegetables and particularly on organic offerings. Vitamin and mineral supplements she was also taking a close look at. Acupuncture and Reiki were both growing in importance. Each of them helped to alleviate both pain and fatigue. The work with her spiritual healer was all about working with the smooth flow of qi through the meridians affecting her heart, her mind, her body, and her spirit. Acupuncture, Reiki, and spiritual healing all contributed to her relearning how to relax into the moment. The work with her lymphedema specialist rounded out her therapeutic treatments. Her spa visits further enhanced her sense of well-being. Her life was very full.

August did roll around. Taking care of first things first, she made an appointment to get her hair trimmed. This appointment she really looked forward to, as it would mark yet another "normal" activity to which she could return. Her former stylist, Rachael, had moved out of the area, but not before prepping a previous co-worker of hers to be ready for Penney's return to the beauty salon. Upon her arrival at the shop, the very talented and rakishly dressed Sam greeted her with a big hug and oodles of compliments on how attractive the white blond/dove gray combo was on her. Penney and Sam together decided to shape and style her hair into a very short pixie and to add just a hint of strawberry-blond highlights. The end result was nothing short of pizzazzy. Jack called it hot!

Penny was still never far from the shadows of her cancer, however, and mid-month found her in a marathon of scans and tests again. Dr. Bradley had consulted with Dr. Anthony in order to have this new look at Penney as comprehensive as possible. Her mammogram showed an area thought benign, but it would continue to be monitored. The CT scan reported the nodules previously discovered in her lungs were stable. The MRI reported evidence of an old childhood injury, but no evidence of metastatic disease was found. One out of three tests showing nothing remarkable was not good enough for Penney.

Meeting with Dr. Bradley, Penney could only think to ask, "What is going on here? Did I have too much chemo, too much radiation? I still have pain around the incision area. Why isn't all this clearing up?" Penney sat wide-eyed, expectantly waiting for a response.

Dr. Bradley looked directly at Penney and replied, "If scans were done routinely on the public at large, numerous nodules would be found. We don't always know why they show up. They do tend to appear as people age. I can tell you that your particular kind of cancer typically does not metastasize this way. Remember also that you are not even six months out of treatment and not even a year from surgery. You're doing well. I might add you are looking much healthier since the last time we met."

"Patience is not always my strong suit. I worry. Am I doing enough? What should I have been doing to prevent all this in the first place? I'm highly sensitive to heat and cold, and tender all over my body. I can't seem to shake this congestion and runny nose." As Penney wiped her nose for the umpteenth time that day, she stopped her litany, peered squarely at Dr. Bradley and announced, "Okay, I'm a mess."

Dr. Bradley reached over to pat Penney lightly on the arm. "You are no different from any other patient I have met regarding your concerns. Believe me, you are doing everything right, and you're doing well. Just keep doing what you are doing. It's impressive, Penney, and has to be contributing to your recovery. I will be leaving here soon, as you know. Dr. Anthony has asked that you follow up with him later in the fall. Be strong, Penney."

They shook hands and wished each other well. Penney walked out to her car with some certainty that she had to give it all more time. With that resolve, Penney turned her thoughts to the high school and the tasks awaiting her there.

Exiting off the highway, Penney could immediately glimpse the construction project. Workers moved in every direction as the project progressed in high gear. There was a new urgency as the upcoming school year loomed just around the corner. One hundred fifty staff would soon return, followed by twelve hundred students. All needed their instructional space. Drawing closer to the school, Penney slowed down. Off in the distance, the football team and the marching band were practicing on the playing fields. Penney decided to drive on out to the fields to view their practices. The energy among the band members was infectious. Penney welcomed them and then took some of their enthusiasm with her as she moved on to watch the football team and to share her hopes for their upcoming season with them. As they returned to their coaches, one young player broke rank and came over to Penney.

"Mrs. Divan, I just want to tell you how proud I am to be playing for you. We all are. Your act is going to be hard to follow, but we're going to make you proud, ma'am."

Penney was overcome with genuine gratitude. As Penney shook his hand, she warmly thanked the young man, who then trotted off to join the practice drills. He faded into the other players.

Well, Penney thought, *I must get stronger for them, as well as for me.* The students had unfailingly rallied around her at all times, but especially during this last year. She watched the practice a little longer and then waved to the coaches, who each, in turn, returned her wave. As she turned her car around toward the summer staff parking lot, she was aware of eyes watching her. She so wanted to live up to everyone's expectations. She most assuredly didn't want to disappoint her students!

Penney now had to find those students an assistant principal. She had gone through all the applications. A few appeared very promising on paper, and these few would be interviewed by her and the department chairs the next day. Penney reviewed the applications again that afternoon, and she did a final inspection of the areas in the building that she planned to share with the candidates. For the most part, she would show them completed spaces, but she also wanted to propose scenarios which involved temporary classrooms and makeshift passageways. Maintaining expectations for everyone in the building during the many construction phases had always been a key priority for Penney. Likewise, the new assistant principals would need to share this priority.

The interviews and the subsequent building tours went well, with one candidate clearly standing out among the others. Penney was able to speak to his references in a very timely fashion. Dr. Ferrari met with him. His family visited the area over the weekend. The school board approved him. He accepted the job immediately when Penney called to make the offer. In just over a week, Penney had a new assistant principal. Dr. Ferrari talked to the other superintendent, and Jon Goldman was sitting at his desk during the staff's return to work at the end of the month.

Jon came with a dozen years of content classroom experience, as well as coaching experience. He was tall, well groomed, and intelligent. He would prove to be an imposing figure. He arrived with innovative ideas to approach discipline and with the energy Penney needed to propel her leadership.

The school year opened with all knowing what needed to happen and how each person would assist in creating an atmosphere of learning within a very active construction site. Both Penney and Jon knew they were doing the principals' roles in tandem, but until another qualified candidate came along, they had agreed they could do it.

Penney was busy during the day at the high school. She rotated her afternoons around athletic events, other school events, and integrative medicine appointments while maintaining a social life complete with jazz and dance concerts, long weekend visits to Manhattan and to California to visit her children and grandchildren, and meeting friends for dinner and occasionally after school for drinks. This dizzying schedule helped Penney to push aside her intermittent pain and to squelch negative feelings when they arose. Her energy and her strength were slowly returning. Her smile never left her face.

The calendar kept moving along. October, of course, brought Penney to the state principals' conference. There she did run into Ted and Angie when rounding a corner on her way to an instructional session. This encounter took her breath away, but she did manage to flash them a smile and to say, "Hey, you two!" as she scurried on, her breath gradually catching up to her. Images floated across Penney's brain of the three of them dancing in the rain and laughing outside her office. That image was quickly displaced by the memory of Ted and Angie laughing as they looked her way and then pointedly turning their backs to her. That old heartache over the loss of their friendship and trust flashed momentarily, followed by the now all-too-familiar pain in her upper left chest area. Penney simply would not allow herself to dwell on either the disquieting meeting or the unwanted sorrow and pain. Ending with crisp days and a bounty of fall color, October left with its own treasures.

November was marked by the traditional parent/teacher conferences and visiting with family at Thanksgiving. Ginger, Ken, and the granddaughters, Annie and Marly, joined them at Jack's mother's home in Mountain View for the anticipated lively holiday visit. Penney and Jack's son, Michael, did not join them, as he struggled with relationship and money worries. He was a growing puzzle to Penney and Jack, but he was pointedly reluctant to share with them. They had to accept that he would come around in his own time. Likewise, Penney's parents remained relatively removed, not really specifying why. Jack's relatives kept them all entertained, leaving little time to dwell on Michael's issues or Penney's parents' reserve. Penney was sure all would be well in time.

November also brought another scan. There was nothing new or noteworthy according to the radiologist. Penney's suspicious pain on the upper left side of her chest was now allegedly due to prior radiation therapy. The nodules formerly reported remained stable. There was nothing remarkable medically in the report, and Penney tried to tell herself stable was good.

Penney's annual holiday trip to the Baja brought a much-needed two weeks of relaxation. Extra sleep was beneficial, there was no doubt. Penney's usual pattern of starting out the week rested, only to find herself slowing down due to fatigue by Wednesday, exhausted by Thursday, and so tired she was physically ill by Friday was interrupted by nights of adequate sleep and enduring energy later in the week.

Penney spent her mornings in the Baja lolling in the sun soaking up the vitamin D. Afternoons found Penney reading leisurely in the shade with many a cool drink. Relaxation was the rule for each day. Jack insisted she take heed. Penney, on the other hand, knew that she and everyone else demanded she work hard. For good measure, Jack surprised her on Christmas Day with a ticket to Paris to accompany him on a business trip in February. He made her promise she would slow down, smell the roses, and put her feet up at least once every day. That would be her gift to him, Jack had decided.

It was now possible to do that a little, she had to admit. Work at the high school was running smoothly. Jon was a good match with Penney, both equally sharing an authoritative and commanding presence. Together they were able to operate a robust school program efficiently and effectively, with very few affected by the construction going on all around them. Sean did continue to help out with discipline a few times a week. Penney had started a subtle campaign to convince Sean to think about joining the ranks of administration. She did, however, fully understand how difficult it could be to step out of the classroom. She was content with the current arrangement for now. Penney was focusing on her upcoming trip to France when she found time to kick her feet up and relax.

The Paris trip was magical, bringing with it a lot of white magic and, alas, a little black magic too. When Jack was in meetings, she took turns rendezvousing with her two Parisian friends, spending a day at the Musée d'Orsay oohing and ahhing over the Impressionists with one and puzzling over the work of Picasso with the other. And the shopping! Ooh-la-la! The House of Chanel alone consumed the better part of an afternoon. Penney tried on dresses that made her feel like French royalty. In the end, she bought a tube of lipstick to remember her afternoon in this world of luxury and fantasy.

For the most part, Penney and Jack did all the touristy things together under cloudy skies, wrapped in the warmth provided by the cloud cover, sweaters, and happy hearts. They looked up at the Eiffel Tower from a tourist-ridden plaza and marveled at the simplicity of its architectural splendor reaching toward the heavens. The walk to the top of the Arc de Triomphe offered a whole new perspective on the Champs-Elysée, one of depth and vastness encompassing the humanity surging along the boulevard below. Sacré Cœur, in all its splendor, rose up amidst a cornflower-blue sky pillowed with white, fluffy clouds. It was a view that made the angels sing in Penney's and Jack's heads, suggesting a power far greater than the two of them. The Louvre added beauty on the inside to a day of drizzle on the outside. No matter how many times Penney had visited the collection of Impressionists at the Louvre or elsewhere, she came away with new insights into how to see the world around her. Her day at the Louvre with Jack did not disappoint. The Left Bank always made the two of them smile. They could feel love in the air there. The large number of embracing couples underscored their impressions. At the Tuileries, Jack took one of his favorite pictures of Penney. In this picture, Penney appeared to be deep in conversation with one of the sculptures. Her head was cocked with her chin resting in her hand, a puzzled look on her face. The food was magnificent as they shared favorite standbys, such as *bœuf bourgignon* and *coq au vin*. The wine, as was to be expected, was divine. Burgundies, both white and red, paired well with the hearty dishes they chose to order. The jazz clubs in the Latin Quarter proved to be out of this world. They danced until the wee hours of the morning more than once.

There was one occasion, though, when the trip flickered. Since Penney's very first chemotherapy treatment, she had struggled with vaginal dryness that left her insides burning following intercourse. She had tried everything over the counter but with very little relief. This condition was making intimacy difficult. Awakening one morning in Paris to a room bathed in the first golden rays of the sun, Penney and Jack made tender love with one another. Penney experienced the usual nips of pain—in, out; in, out; in, ouch!—and squirmed a little in the beginning, but compensated for it by totally throwing herself into the lovemaking, breathing deeply when the jabs of pain took her breath away for a second. However, when Jack gave her a final kiss and rose from the bed, he announced, "Penney, I know that is uncomfortable for you. I don't want to hurt you after all that you have been through, so we're not going to do this anymore." With that, he went to shower and prepare for his day.

Penney's eyes flooded with tears, and she rolled over to muffle her sobs. Penney knew all too well that Jack hated it when she cried. Before he left for the day, he kissed the back of her head and said, "Penney, I do love you more than you will ever know. Remember, I'll be late tonight." As the door shut behind him, Penney could only focus on one thought: *One more door closes, but where will the next one open?*

She walked the streets of Paris by herself that day, feeling empty and utterly alone. The February chill sliced right through her. Jack's resolve to help her heal without enjoying intimacy caused one more heartstring to break and dangle in the wind. Penney would have to keep a keen eye out for the magic once again. She knew it did indeed await her discovery; she had only to observe. With that, although the City of Lights had dimmed, Penney still tried to drink in the joys of the city, just perhaps a little less voraciously. Later in the week, when she tried to broach the subject, Jack stood firm and would not discuss possible solutions. Penney was certain that in Jack's mind, he did not love Penney less, but rather more. He would make this sacrifice for Penney. Her self-esteem was waffling, she knew, but there was no one else she really wanted to share this with. This was a stalemate she had not anticipated nor expected. With the beauty of Paris revolving around her newfound darkness, she resolved to win back the love she felt she had lost. Penney would not abandon hope. Jack was her best friend when all was said and done.

Once home, Penney and Jack prepared for a visit from Ginger and Ken. Penney took a day off from work for their long weekend visit so that she could really enjoy the visit and to rest. Try as they might, her alternative medicine practitioners were having a devil of a time fighting her intermittent pain, her on-again, off-again fatigue, and her pensiveness. When they conferred, they all agreed Penney didn't seem like her usual self. Penney knew they were right. Seeing

Ginger made her relax a little. When they sat down to talk, they both reminded one another that they had always fantasized about taking a mother-daughter trip to Greece. Investigating together, they discovered a little village overlooking the Ionian Sea that sounded perfect. They would continue to explore this possibility for a tentative autumn excursion. The visit was short, though, and all returned to business as usual.

For Penney, that meant more scans and tests. These would be in her life forever, she was told, so she was trying to learn to accept this reality. She did them all in one day—mammogram, PET/CT scan, and MRI. She ended the day at the spa getting a manicure and pedicure. She looked good on the outside and hoped against hope that she looked good on the inside as well. She still wondered at the PET scan arrangement moving back and forth from the emergency room waiting area and traversing icy walkways to do so. She would meet with Dr. Anthony next week, a treacherous path itself, to explore the results with him.

In the meantime, there were state tests to administer to the juniors in the high school. This particular class of juniors should do well, as they were a pretty bright group of kids. This was not always the case with each different class every year. Penney also had a suicide prevention training to participate in. This turned out to be loaded with valuable information concerning teen suicide, which she would share with her staff at their next in-service training. Over the weekend, both Penney and Jack attended a scholarship fund-raising dinner, which benefitted the senior class every year to the tune of tens of thousands of dollars. It was also a fun dinner with dancing at the end.

Penney arrived a little early for her appointment with Dr. Anthony. She wanted time to breathe before asking him her questions. After a twenty-minute wait, she was escorted to the exam room by the pudgy nurse who talked nonstop about anything that popped into her head. Penney wallowed a little in the silence as the nurse pulled the door shut. Penney changed into the ever-glamorous gown and waited some more. Dr. Anthony entered the room with his head bent over her reports.

"Uh, hi. These say pretty much the same. Still no explanation for your chest pain. Like I have said before, the changes reported are all due to your surgery and, the tests suggest, could also be due to your treatments." Dr. Anthony set the reports down on the desk, looked up at Penney, and crossed his arms across his chest. "So there you have it. Nothing new."

"Do they still refer to the activity in my left chest wall as a possible neoplasm?"

"Radiologists just use that term to cover themselves. It's still status quo."

"Are there no additional things that could be done to entirely rule out a tumor?"

"Not warranted. You need to give it all some time to heal."

"But it has been quite a while…"

"We've got time. Now, let's take a look."

As usual during the physical exam, Penney drew in her breath at the mere touch to her chest. "That really is painful."

"With the treatments you had, I would not be surprised at this sensitivity to touch. I want to see you in six months and we'll have some more tests done then." With that, he left the room.

"For whoever might care, this really is not the way I should be healing," she said out loud. Penney knew some spirit somewhere had heard her. Not sure if she should be discouraged or start thinking she was going mad, she checked out, asking for a copy of the reports. Penney walked slowly to her car, ruminating all the way. *Well, here I am, alone and missing information again. God, this is frustrating!*

She sat down with Jack that evening to go over the reports. There it all was indeed. The nodules were still resting comfortably, but there was increased activity in the left chest wall. "Call me crazy if you want, but doesn't this suggest I'm right? Something simply is not right." Penney was understandably exasperated.

"Penney, you are not crazy. We will give it a little more time, but maybe you need to see another doctor." Penney could not help noticing that Jack was more than a bit puzzled and worry was seeping into his psyche. They both called it a night, but their sleep was fretful.

The calendar kept ticking away, the months continuing to rapidly roll into one another. In April, Penney took Jack to San Antonio to celebrate his sixtieth birthday. Penney had asked Jack why San Antonio when he could choose any place in the world. He had replied that when he was a young boy, Davy Crockett had been one of his heroes. There seemed to be some mystery surrounding Crockett's death at the Alamo. He thought it might be interesting for the two of them to investigate. Penney was game. It sounded like fun!

Penney and Jack landed in San Antonio on a warm afternoon in April. They stowed their luggage in the trunk of their rental car. Driving to their hotel, they both noted the comfortably warm temperatures. They were also intrigued by the natural vegetation, a combination of oak and cedar woodlands with a grassy savanna and chaparral brush. Once checked into the hotel, Penney and Jack took a leisurely walk along the famed River Walk. The waterways flowed gently beside the walking path and its resplendent vegetation and numerous brightly colored flowers. Over two miles long, the River Walk afforded Penney and Jack their customary daily walk amidst an unparalleled urban park complete with upscale restaurants and shopping. Penney and Jack chose one of the many fine Tex-Mex restaurants to enjoy some local specialties. The two of them dug right into *pollo con rajas de chile ancho,* savoring the cacophony of flavors. The *tamal de chocolate* proved to be a truly luscious dessert. As they dined, Penney and Jack watched other tourists meander along the walkways and skim the waterways in boats.

The next morning found Penney and Jack standing across the street photographing the Mission San Antonio de Valero, once a Roman Catholic mission turned fortress compound where the Battle of the Alamo was fought. Today, it appeared as a stately Spanish mission building, though not at all imposing in its present-day urban setting. Penney and Jack wandered through the site but found no definitive answers to their query concerning Crockett's demise. They looked over historical registers and personal accounts of the conflict. They quizzed the docents. In the final analysis, the historians were still puzzled. Penney and Jack were not to settle whether Crockett died in the siege or was taken prisoner and executed on Santa Anna's direct orders. Privately, Penney was leaning toward capture and execution. She was not sharing that with Jack, as he was leaning toward Crockett dying valiantly in the defense of the Alamo. When all was said and done, they had enjoyed their foray together into historical research.

What Penney and Jack did discover was that the Mission Trail in the San Antonio Missions National Park offered a great walking experience for a couple of days while soaking up the history of the area. Each of the remaining four missions on the trail, Penney and Jack learned, reflected the lives of the people in this area during Spanish occupation. Penney and Jack concluded that the city of San Antonio had much to be proud of, as the missions were well preserved and the residents were dedicated to maintaining the old missions and the new River Walk to enchant tourists and natives alike.

It was a healthy diversion for the two of them, walking during the day and dancing at night. The fresh air, sunshine, fact-finding, and dancing, however, did not lead to the intimacy Penney was now gravely missing. Jack still would not entertain a discussion on the topic. He left on a business trip to Asia as soon as they returned home.

Penney's days, as usual, were filled with work, student activities, and myriad appointments. Jon was an actual dream come true. Their synchronicity never failed to astound Penney. She did the bulk of the teacher observations, while Jon oversaw most of the student discipline. Penney kept a finger on the pulse of the construction project. Together, they worked to further their efforts in instructional leadership.

Alas, the pain in her left chest area grew more pronounced and more frequent and could no longer be ignored. Penney could now feel tiny lumps in the area around her incision site. An appointment with Nell, her lymphedema specialist, confirmed she was not hallucinating.

"You know, Penney, this feels different, almost hard here," speculated Nell with worry clearly in her voice.

"Uggh! I know. It hurts almost all the time, too. What do you think it is?" parried Penney.

"When do you see Dr. Anthony? I think he should see this." Nell's brow was creased and her constant smile not in evidence.

"I just saw him a few weeks ago, and he indicated everything was stable. He pretty much implied he thought my pain was all in my head." Penney sighed deeply.

"I don't think I can agree with him. It's not like you to complain. If you say it hurts, I'm certain it hurts. Let's see if we can't get you in to see him."

Before Penney left Nell's office, the appointment with Dr. Anthony was made for the following week. In the meantime, the pain increased. When Penney did see Dr. Anthony, he thought it just might be scar tissue she was feeling. He believed, as he had persistently maintained, that this area was simply residuals from the lumpectomy he had performed. Yet, in the end, he agreed a biopsy was probably now warranted.

Jack returned from his business trip to learn that Penney was scheduled for a surgical biopsy the following Monday. Penney could plainly see Jack's concern was hard to cover up. Penney herself was numb. Yet, forever trying to keep life moving forward, Penney had arranged to meet friends for dinner that weekend. These were the very same friends they had dined with prior to Penney learning of her initial cancer diagnosis. Indeed, could this be déjà vu? The evening was enjoyable, and nothing was mentioned about the pending biopsy. Sunday was quiet, though both Jack and Penney were nervous.

Very early Monday morning, Penney checked in to the outpatient surgery center without incident. She was prepped for surgery and whisked off to the operating room. As Penney came out of the anesthesia in the recovery room, Jack hovered over her, concern now clearly written all over his face. Penney offered him a weak smile and whispered, "Pain…"

A nurse flew over and asked, "On a scale of one to ten, with ten being the worst pain you have experienced, where would you say your pain is?"

Through gritted teeth, Penney answered, "Nine. Nine." The pain seemed to be eating away at her chest. She clutched Jack's hand and rolled back and forth on the bed.

Pain medication was immediately given. Both nurses in attendance looked at one another in alarm. As the edge to the pain began to taper, Dr. Anthony came flying into the recovery area. His eyes were as big as saucers, accentuated by his round glasses frames. All color was drained from his face. He nervously clenched a paper in his hand.

"The preliminary lab results suggest your cancer is back! It's in the muscle, and you are going to need more surgery!" He talked hurriedly, sounding almost crazed.

Jack looked dumbfounded. Penney started to cry even as the pain medication began to shut down her senses. Her eyes fluttered as her cheeks were dampened by her tears. Jack took both her hands and squeezed tight. Dr. Anthony turned and almost ran out of the room, shaking his head in disbelief as he balled up the paper in his hand. Penney fell into a deep, medicated sleep, thrashing in the bed and moaning. It was not until much later in the day that she was able to be released from the surgery center. Jack carefully tucked her into bed when they returned home. He realized he was angry but was not sure where to direct his anger. He sat in the kitchen staring out as he watched the night take over.

V

Penney worked from home the next morning and was at her desk in the high school that afternoon. She was visibly tired, her under-eye cream not even close to covering up the dark circles under her eyes. Unusually quiet, Penney labored primarily on paperwork. The few people she met received polite, reserved responses to their concerns. When she returned home, Penney changed into her pajamas and continued her e-mail and paperwork propped up in bed. Work had always kept her going before, and she vowed to maintain her commitment to her role. This cancer thing was not going to derail her.

The follow-up appointment with Dr. Anthony later in the week was actually anticlimactic. Penney had known in her heart for over a year that something was not quite right. While feeling somewhat vindicated, she also felt like her body, the one she worked so hard at fixing and keeping in shape, was continually letting her down. *Why? Oh, why?* she had to keep asking herself. What she did articulate to Dr. Anthony was that she needed an oncologist who knew something about her cancer, this bizarre form of triple negative cancer called metaplastic carcinoma. She would travel up to two hours to see this person, who had to be prepared to give her choices. Dr. Anthony still seemed stunned at the biopsy's results and complacently agreed to investigate her requests. He also wrote orders for her to have another

CT scan, as well as a bone scan. The new doctor would need this information.

Graduation week was upon her. Like many things about her role as principal, Penney was able to pull off each event with grace because each was thankfully familiar. Awards night found her beaming as she watched the majority of her graduating seniors walking off the stage with monies, recognitions, and ultimately expectations for them to do well and succeed in life. Friday evening at graduation, as she addressed her seniors and their relatives, friends, and community members, Penney paused over a carefully chosen quotation.

"Emily Dickinson once said, 'To live is so startling it leaves little time for anything else.'"

Penney gazed at the crowd gathered before her and silently reaffirmed her conviction to live and to live largely. Her smiles and well-wishes as each senior passed by her on the stage were tokens of hope for all their futures, including her own. A couple of the seniors danced her across the stage and brought a joyful laugh to join her smile. Penney was going to face this new battle with determination.

During that same week, amidst awards and graduation, Penney visited Dr. Anthony one last time. He had the name of an oncologist to give her. He had met with this oncologist personally, and he was eager to share that the oncologist not only knew about metaplastic carcinoma, but also fully understood Penney wanted to be given options. While Dr. Anthony's staff set up the appointment, he and Penney went over the results of the CT scan and the bone scan. The CT scan confirmed a recurrence—*More like "Oops! Didn't get it all the first time,"* Penney couldn't help thinking. There was no further evidence of metastatic disease found in the bone scan. Before Penney left Dr. Anthony's office that day, she had an appointment to meet with Dr. Catrina Salvatore. Dr. Salvatore was located outside of Clochebarre in the town of Sirrah Glen. When Penney explained all this to Jack, he was a little hesitant about the distance, but if this was what Penney wanted, then so be it. Penney saw Jack off Sunday morning at the airport to begin a business trip to Greece. Meanwhile,

Penney waited for Thursday and the appointment with Dr. Salvatore to happen.

During the intervening days, Penney moved into her new office. She had watched it materialize out of the wreckage of demolition. It was as she had envisioned it: spacious, inviting, with plants and a massive picture window with a tree planted outside of it, comfy furnishings, and numerous black-and-white photos of Paris—homey. It was interesting and disconcerting that Paris portended so much loss for her when it symbolized eternal life for her as well in many ways. She would be seeing to it that the beauty of life triumphed. Penney also started the summer projects for the high school and informed Frank and the summer office staff about what was going on with her. Penney could see the concern and the letdown in their faces. She would see these same looks in many faces over the next several months.

Thursday dawned with a hint of summer warmth. Penney meditated, exercised, and dressed for the day. Her nearly two-hour drive to Dr. Salvatore's office was uneventful and seemed shorter than it really was. She checked in, filled out the cursory paperwork, and surveyed the waiting room. It looked like someone's solarium. Plants dotted the walls, and wicker furniture was arranged in conversational settings. In fact, nurses would come out to sit beside a patient and conversations did take place.

Penney was escorted back to the exam area by a slightly built woman who identified herself as Karla. She weighed Penney, took her temperature, and introduced her to Franny, the phlebotomist. Franny was buxom, pleasant, smiley, and chatty. She quickly but deftly found a vein in Penney's right arm from which to draw blood. Penney then returned to the waiting area for only a short time before Karla returned to escort her to an exam room.

Penney donned the all-too-familiar gown. *Someone seems to have cornered the gown market.* The room itself, though, was furnished with traditional dark wood furniture complementing the sage-colored walls and pumpkin-flecked carpeting. *Inviting and professional in every aspect so far.* A tap on the door, and it was opened by Dr. Salvatore, a woman of medium height, slim, waves of dark curls cascading to her shoulders, her lab coat open to reveal a summer-weight linen suit in navy with brilliant red wedge heels on her feet. Her smile filled the room as she extended her hand to Penney.

"Penney, I am pleased to meet you. I'm Dr. Salvatore. I understand from my conversations with Dr. Anthony that you and I have some choices to discuss and some work ahead for the two of us."

"I am happy to meet you as well," replied Penney, feeling a little of her usual stress in these situations beginning to slip away.

"I spent most of the evening going over your file. You will be my first triple-negative patient. As I am sure you know, your hormone tests are all essentially negative. Triple negative cancer has been getting quite a bit of attention recently. Your metaplastic carcinoma is just one of many triple negative cancers, though it is far more rare than many of the others. This makes you a special challenge, but I hear you are up for challenges. Let's have a look at you, and then we can explore a few choices together."

The physical exam was very thorough. Dr. Salvatore even measured the tumor. She asked Penney to get dressed before they talked, respectfully leaving the room while Penney put herself back together. *This is unbelievable!* Penney thought. *She actually talks to me rather than at me. And everything is so efficient!*

When Dr. Salvatore returned, she went over Penney's blood work, which showed that Penney's white blood cell count continued to be low. Penney's blood pressure, on the other hand, read excellent. Dr. Salvatore then explained that in Penney's case, chemotherapy would precede surgery. She was hoping that a carefully chosen chemo regimen would shrink and soften the tumor, and with the right targeted therapy, they would begin to starve the tumor. The discussion went back and forth, with Penney an equal participant. Dr. Salvatore quickly realized she had one savvy patient in front of her as Penney described why she believed palliative chemotherapy with the standard regimens appeared to be ineffective in the literature. In the final analysis, the two women mutually agreed that a combination of Abraxane and Avastin would be their treatment of choice.

"Now, there may be one issue. Avastin has only very recently been approved for use with breast cancer. Your insurance may not have approved it as of yet. And I can tell you it is expensive."

"I am prepared to assume that expense myself if necessary. I would ask that you check with my insurance first, however, because my coverage is pretty good."

"Okay. You just sit tight. I'll return when I know a little more."

Penney prepared to read for a while when Dr. Salvatore tapped on the door. "I wanted you to meet our insurance coordinator, Mia."

Mia stuck her head in the door to say, "Hi! We're going to look into this for you. Can we get you some coffee or tea while you wait?"

"No, thank you. I'm good for now." Not accustomed to this kind of service or attention in a medical office, Penney was caught a little off guard.

Dr. Salvatore added, "If you change your mind, just let the girls know. We'll be back as quick as we can." She flashed her smile and quietly shut the door.

Penney did not know quite what to do with this feeling of being cared for in a doctor's office. She squirmed a little in her seat and then took a few deep breaths. She needed to be taken care of. They knew this, and so did she.

Not even ten minutes later, Dr. Salvatore quickly poked her head in to say, "It's looking good!" with a thumbs-up.

Another five minutes and both Dr. Salvatore and Mia entered the room, smiling from ear to ear. "Your insurance approved it yesterday!"

"We would like you to start tomorrow if you could," said Dr. Salvatore.

"All right! I'll pick my husband up at the airport tonight and return tomorrow." Penney was grinning now too.

"I would like you to meet the chemo nurses today if you have time. They can give you a quick overview of what to expect tomorrow."

"That would be marvelous! There's just one more thing I need to discuss."

Penney thanked Mia, and Dr. Salvatore came into the room and sat down. "Okay. I'm all yours."

"I travel, a lot actually. I have a trip to Greece planned with my daughter in late summer. And I occasionally join my husband on his business trips. This travel is very important to me."

"So, you shall travel. You will have no hair when you go to Greece, I am afraid."

"Ah! I have a bounty of beautiful scarves to wear. I'm fine with no hair, for a while, anyway."

"Then let's get you started with the nurses today. We will all work around your travel."

Penney followed Dr. Salvatore to the chemotherapy suite. There she was introduced to the staff at the nurses' station and then sat down with the nurse, Tess, who would oversee her care. They sat in a room the size of a small bedroom furnished with comfortable chairs and tables, good lighting, TV, Wi-Fi, and chemo monitors. Penney nearly fell off her chair when she learned that each patient was assigned to a private room like this to receive treatment. She was told that many of their patients led very busy lives and often worked from these rooms. Penney was thinking it would take her no time at all to get used to this.

The next order of business was to go over the prescriptions she would be using. Abraxane was essentially a high-dose paclitaxel designed to reduce tumors. Avastin, not chemotherapy but rather an anti-angiogenic therapy, would be attacking the blood vessels feeding the tumor. Each infusion would be relatively quick compared to her earlier experience. She would lose her hair, experience fatigue, and probably have nosebleeds from time to time. They would be carefully monitoring her blood cell count, her blood pressure, and the protein in her urine. Both of these medications were proving to be well tolerated by patients, who reported very few side effects, in large part because there were no solvents included in their formulations. That meant that there would be no pre-medications given, as nausea and swollen eyes and lips were all solvent-related toxicities. The drugs

Penney would be given did not use chemicals to dissolve for their administration.

"Wow!" said Penney. "I have also been reading that the temporary neuropathy I could experience, as well as some of the fatigue, will probably be offset by my exercise routines."

"True. You exercise a lot?"

"A little…" Penney quietly offered, stifling a giggle.

Tess shot her a smile.

Thinking it needed to be mentioned, Penney added, "During my last round with chemo, my alternative care providers, principally my acupuncturist, fought a relentless battle with nausea. I want to be absolutely sure I won't have that same war to wage. Sometimes it was not pretty."

"I will talk to Dr. Salvatore about your concern, and we'll be ready to fight the good fight tomorrow. Now, don't you have a plane to meet?"

When Penney left Dr. Salvatore's office that day, she felt strangely empowered—in charge, actually. She sang along with her loud music most of the trip home, arriving with only minutes to spare before Jack's plane set down.

Penney went up to him with open arms. Jack dropped his things and wrapped his arms around her. They stood there hugging one another for a long, long time. Others walked around them and smiled; a few hugged their mates in turn.

"I missed you!" Jack declared as he looked Penney over from arm's length. "I'm guessing the appointment went well…"

"Jack, I was treated like a person. It was nice. I think I will be in good hands." Penney proceeded to give Jack a detailed report of her visit to Dr. Salvatore's office as they gathered his things and his luggage and made their way home. Though not intimate, it was a tenderhearted and loving evening.

Bright and early, Penney and Jack hit the road to Sirrah Glen. When Penney asked Jack to accompany her, he had not hesitated. In fact, there was no discussion. It had been understood during her previous treatments that Jack would not be a participant. Penney knew to take each new treatment one at a time. For this first new treatment, she was relieved to have his company, his presence. The skies surrounding them were clear and blue, the highway free of heavy traffic, and Jack's occasional squeezing of her hand sweet.

Tess met them in the waiting area, coming to sit with the two of them to be introduced to Jack. As they all walked back to the chemo area, Tess showed them where they could help themselves to coffee, tea, juices, water, and healthy snacks. When they entered Penney's own private room for the next few hours, Jack's look of surprise at how well outfitted the room was let Penney know he would be okay for today. They each opened their laptops and had their cell phones within arm's reach. Tess found a viable vein in Penney's right arm and prepared it for infusion while going over the procedures with Jack. She added, too, that as a result of her talking to Dr. Salvatore about Penney's concern regarding nausea, they would be beginning with steroids and Aloxi as a precautionary measure. Penney was pleased they had considered her input but sorry she would probably have to suffer through some side effects now with these pre-medications. Tess brought blankets and pillows for Penney and ice water for both Penney and Jack.

The pre-meds took about thirty minutes, the Abraxane another thirty, and the Avastin an additional ninety minutes. It was best to settle in and get some work done. The time seemed to pass fairly quickly as Penney and Jack worked while Tess unobtrusively kept a watchful eye on Penney. There were a tense several moments when Tess speeded up the drip at one point. This brought on an immediate rapid heart rate. Penney felt creepy, like bugs were crawling over her, as a consequence, and her shoulders were very tense once her heart rate was brought down. As always when Penney was stressed, she was overcome with a teeth-chattering chill. Jack piled on the warm blankets Tess brought in the room and closed his laptop for a while. Otherwise, the first treatment was uneventful. Penney and Jack ate a late lunch at a nearby restaurant and then headed home. Penney slept peacefully in the car on the ride home while Jack reflected on their afternoon together.

Once settled at home, he had to ask, "Is that pretty much how it went before, Penney?"

"Well, this was several times more comfortable and blissfully quiet."

"I mean the infusion process—finding a vein, watching the meds drip, you know…"

"Yep, it's how it goes. This was much shorter than most of my treatments from before, in large part because I was not made to wait. And Tess is so pleasant. She explains things, answers questions, and seems to actually be interested in how I am doing. The thing with the heart rate she addressed immediately. That is very different from previously."

"Gosh, Penney, I really didn't have any idea. I don't know if I could carry through with all this. How often do you do this?"

"Every other week for a while, my friend." Penney looked at Jack thoughtfully, gauging whether she should broach the topic of his future participation.

Jack continued as she pondered, "So, how toxic are these drugs, Penney?"

"They need to reduce the size of the tumor, Jack, so pretty toxic."

"Your nurse said you shouldn't be as sick as you were before."

"I'm kinda counting on that, Jack. I am going to Greece, remember."

"I'm thinking I should go with you now."

"Not possible. It's a mother-daughter only trip."

"I don't know. You will have had quite a bit of these drugs by then."

"Ah, but I know that I'm going. Not open for discussion." Penney batted her eyes and smiled at Jack. Shaking his head, Jack smiled back at her.

"Okay. Let's talk about what you want to eat for dinner and then think about what we might want to do while we are on Long Island next week."

"Oh my gosh! I have had so much on my mind that I haven't given Long Island much thought."

Jack thought to himself, *That's my girl! I'll keep her occupied planning trips. She loves doing that. Maybe I'll take her with me to Kuala Lumpur. Hmmm...*

Over dinner, they studied a map and website for Long Island. They figured out that they wanted to travel out to the Hamptons, tour the Gold Coast mansions and gardens, visit each of the famous lighthouses at Montauk, Fire Island, and Horton Point, and sample the latest vintages at the local vineyards. Friends would be joining them midweek. Most of all, they both knew they needed to just rest. While rest was a priority, Penney and Jack were also seasoned travelers. They slept in each day while on Long Island while still managing to take in a major sightseeing destination each day.

Also devoted to their work, Penney and Jack kept up with their e-mail—granted, in rather relaxed settings—during their days on Long Island. Penney was now waging a very serious campaign for Sean to come onboard as vice principal. Jon was right behind her, reinforcing and reiterating each of her rationales in person while Penney delivered them via e-mail, blind copying Jon with each well-thought-out rationale for Sean to join them at this time. Penney knew surgery was in her future, and although no specifics had as yet been discussed, she knew the surgery would be major. Penney needed Sean now.

When their friends, Doug and Kate, joined them on Long Island, they all together mutually agreed to still sleep in, partake of leisurely lunches in quiet seaside villages, and ramble up and down the coastline, awed by its stark simplicity and beauty. One evening, while walking barefoot on the beach to catch a truly breathtaking sunset, Kate asked Penney if she was enjoying her short hair.

Penney came to an abrupt halt in the sand, sending shimmery slivers up to catch the last rays of the sun. She took in Kate's perfectly coiffed, shoulder-length blonde hair also highlighted by the sunset. "Well...I have been. It's easy to care for, fun to style, and great for traveling. But, but...you do realize it all goes next week, right?" Penney was trying not to be flabbergasted, but the timing of the question seemed a little off. She supposed she was being a little overly sensitive.

"Sure, but I was thinking about having my hair cut a little shorter, so I was curious. I think I would miss pulling it back in a ponytail, though, so I don't know if I will go through with it."

Penney's heart kept sinking lower and lower. She knew she had up to twenty-one days before her hair would completely fall out. She knew she should just blow this off. Her hair would grow back. She simply could not imagine being on the delivery end of this conversation, however. Penney still missed her long hair and having it braided. Not trusting her cancer, though, Penney had chosen not to let her hair grow out much. Her hair had been such a defining feature of hers previously. Now she had to give up her new hair look. To top it off, she now also had to defend her new short hair knowing that she would have her head shaved in a few days. Kate droned on about what style might look best and how much hair she might have trimmed. Penney was working hard to keep a smile on her face and to not feel sorry for herself. Jack was keying in to her distress and wisely changed the topic to focus on what they all might do that evening. Slowly, Penney could feel that cold, white knot of nothing in her stomach begin to abate. *It's just hair! It's just hair! It's just hair!* The week and the visit with Doug and Kate ended well, with no more panic buttons being pushed.

Penney returned to work the next week rested. She was also mentally prepared for her buzz cut that Tuesday. The conversation with her friend Kate, she had to admit, had prepared her for this loss. She was able to explain to Sam matter-of-factly what she wanted done and why. He valiantly protested, pleading with her to let him color it hot pink for a couple of weeks. Penney stayed firm. Once Sam had shaved her head, he then handed the clippers to Penney and had her shave his head. The entire beauty salon cheered them on, admiring their handiwork. Scarf carefully tied on her head, Penney left the salon with a hug from Sam and with a strong sense that she needed to move ahead for her and her alone, at least initially. Her original experience with cancer had left her stranded in a sea of distant observers. She knew they would be watching again and waiting to see how she fared this time around. Penney was familiar with the dance steps, and by golly, she would twirl for all to see, but especially to emerge a better and stronger person for herself foremost.

Penney had asked Sean to meet her early the next morning. She was pretty certain the scarf look would help her persuasive arguments along. It did. Sean had given her pleas a lot of serious consideration before this meeting, and he was ready to commit to assist this woman wherever and however he could. They mutually agreed he would join her administrative team the first of August. This would allow him some vacation time before he hit the ground running. Penney took Jon and Sean out for lunch to celebrate. This was all beginning to feel much better. As always, having people and things in place made Penney feel more secure. She had been doing a lot of work with animal totems with her spiritual healer, Rita. This work was centered around protecting herself (leopard), stabilizing her power position (raven), moving cautiously and with care (turtle), and staying strong for what was to come (coyote). Penney felt that she was heeding these messages.

Before beginning the long Independence Day weekend in Manhattan, Penney and Jack made their second treatment trip to Sirrah Glen. It was on their way, so Penney didn't even have to negotiate Jack's coming along. They worked side by side together again while the drugs did their thing. It was still a three-hour treatment, as they had learned during the first trip that they needed to proceed cautiously with the pacing of the Avastin. Penney also had to report mild queasiness, hot flashes, headaches, congestion, and an occasional nosebleed. She did take advantage of the time to ask privately about vaginal dryness. This treatment center actually had a nurse on duty who dealt solely with questions regarding intimacy. The conversation was educational, but the bottom line was that Penney needed to consider some low-dose estrogen if she ever wanted to be comfortable again. This, it turned out, would be a lasting side effect. Slightly crushed but determined as ever, Penney walked out of that meeting with a prescription.

When they arrived in Manhattan later that day, Jack settled Penney in for a nap while he went for a walk. His thoughts were weighing him down as he blindly walked the streets of midtown. Penney didn't appear to be sick, but he understood this recurrence was huge. This time, he had to honestly admit he was eminently concerned. She hadn't said much, but he did know that not only was Penney frightened, but he was also. *Damn this cancer!* Had he done the right thing to insist that she go through that initial chemo treatment? She had been so ill and was now so thin. The chemo hadn't even killed all the cancer. *Jeez! This is really getting old…*

Jack returned to the room to find Penney smiling and dressed to the nines. *She always looked fabulous in purple!* He took her out to a restaurant he knew she loved, one of those funky little French places. They dined on escargot and *coquilles Saint Jacques* and laughed a lot. Their evening ended at one of their favorite jazz haunts. After a weekend of fireworks, museum hopping, and long walks in the park, they returned home seemingly normal.

Although Sean would not begin his new job until August, he was a key player again in bringing in the master class schedule. Both Jon and Sean worked on the discipline report for the state. Penney oversaw each of these projects and reworked the teachers' evaluation forms, incorporating many of her own initiatives. Dr. Ferrari stopped by the high school personally more often now to be sure Penney was not overdoing it. He knew the high school needed her, but he didn't want it killing her. Penney kept assuring him she was fine and showing him the finishing touches of the construction project.

The final crowning gem of this project had to be the library. The low shelves allowed for total visibility, even into the adjoining computer labs. Each section of the library was set off with practical but comfortable furniture spaced so that whole class groups could be instructed, with as many as a dozen classes able to be in the library at once without disturbing one another. It was one of Penney's favorite spots in the whole building. For the summer, it was used by the various departments holding meetings to discuss courses, and occasionally the school board would use it for their meetings. Penney was anxious to see it filled with her students and their teachers.

Each person coming into the building during the summer and seeing Penney once again in her scarf was openly dismayed. It was not unusual for them to ask a common question: "After all that stuff you've been doing, you still have cancer?" Only Penney understood that all that "stuff" was what was keeping her alive. Dr. Salvatore applauded Penney's team. The team—spiritual healer, acupuncturist, Reiki master/masseuse, lymphedema specialist—conferred from time to time by group conference calls. They were counting on their combined expertise to give Penney the strength she would need to persevere. Like Jack, the team knew in their hearts that this new journey would be fraught with uncalculated risks. For Penney's part, her workouts grew in intensity as she drove herself to keep moving. Medically, the tumor had already shrunk a little, and the pain had abated somewhat—both positive signs. Things appeared to be moving ahead on all fronts.

Yet, Penney wrestled in her mind intermittently with the meaning of this new part of her journey. Where did the wind want to take her, and how was she to face, embrace, erase her fear? She worried, worried, worried. Dr. Salvatore was a gift, yes, but Penney knew they had all entered uncharted waters. The fatigue was already setting in, and this headache! Lord! It was relentless, though it did distract her from her chest wall pain. As she closed her eyes to breathe and visualize these thoughts floating away, Jack entered her office.

"Hey, Beautiful! You meditating on the job?"

Penney's eyes popped open. There was Jack. Jack hardly ever came to see her at work, let alone spontaneously. Penney's mouth opened to say "Hi" as she sat back in her chair. "What's up?"

"I just thought I would bring these by, since you won't have a lot of time to get ready." He handed Penney an envelope.

Penney tore it open and held up two tickets to Kuala Lumpur, surprise slowly lending a pleased glow to her face. She jumped up and moved to Jack to give him a hug. At that moment, Jon and Sean popped up behind Jack.

"Glad you finally got around to giving her those. She hadn't said anything, so we were wondering," quipped Jon. Both men were grinning like schoolboys caught with forbidden goods.

"I wanted to get all the paperwork cleared with Frank first. I have come directly from his office. He does need your signature here, Penney. Then you're off to Malaysia with me."

Penney looked at all three of them with dismay as she moved back to her seat and plopped down. Grinning as well now, she said, "Wow! Let me sign that form, and I'll be nearly ready to go."

"You don't have to worry about a thing while you're away, Mrs. D. The secretaries have already vowed to keep us in line," said Sean. He added, "We have all the major projects done, thanks to you, Mrs. D, so we can't get into too much trouble anyway."

"Good to know! It sounds like you are all in cahoots! So all I have to think about is what to pack. Hmmm… Thanks, guys!" She beamed her signature smile at each of them, but for Jack, she did cock her head a bit. She had to wonder if he was keeping an eye on her—or was he making up for something, or maybe trying to make a point?

Penney and Jack left together, stopping at a favorite restaurant to celebrate on their way home. They toasted one another with champagne and enjoyed a leisurely dinner while looking over the brochures describing Kuala Lumpur that Jack had picked up at AAA on his way to the high school. Penney did remind Jack at one point that she was still traveling to Greece on her own. Jack nodded an affirmative and refocused Penney's attention on the map they had open on the table. They were both really looking forward to this trip by the time dinner was complete.

Now to get ready… Penney would need to see her lymphedema specialist, acupuncturist, Reiki master, and spiritual healer; spend a few hours at the spa; and get in her next chemo treatment before she left, as well as set up these same appointments for after she returned home. She did have a few projects at the high school to point in the right direction, anticipating the late-summer opening of school. Jon and Sean kept reminding her that she had nothing to worry about. Just for good measure, her side effects from the treatments were starting to really kick in: rash from head to toe, abdominal uneasiness, increasing nosebleeds, aches all over, and occasional blue feelings, to name a few. Fatigue, too, could be overwhelming. At work, though, it was business as usual as Penney grew increasingly ill. Nobody ever asked her how she was doing or what she might need, but they all let her know how they were doing and what they needed. Penney had grown accustomed to working out her own needs around them. At the moment, she needed to prepare for this trip.

In the midst of her preparations, however, Tony Snow died. This event gave her pause. Penney had long respected his work as the White House press secretary, and then as journalist and political commentator. She had been following his battle with cancer, in part because his was reportedly an aggressive cancer also, which he appeared to be handling with grace and with dignity. *Pouf! No more! An incomprehensible loss, and why?* Cancer made no sense. *What is the message here? The purpose?* Worry was trying to rear its ugly head again. Her tears were for the loss of Tony, the man, and for her own fears, the demons.

Two days before Penney was to leave, she had treatment and met with Dr. Salvatore, who had a tentative plan to share. Dr. Salvatore anticipated that there would be four to six cycles of Abraxane and Avastin. Penney was beginning her second cycle, so the treatments would continue through the summer. Surgery would follow, so Penney needed to start looking into surgeons. The extent of the surgery was yet to be determined. Following surgery, Penney was to expect more chemo and maybe some radiation. Penney was glad to hear radiation was tenuous, as her previous experience with the radiation team did not predispose her to want anything to do with another foray into radiation. Actually, the whole plan was sketchy and scary. There were too many questions and cautions yet to explore. True, the tumor was marginally smaller and softer. The pain in her chest wall was diminished as well. The side effects from the treatment sucked, however. More of the same on the other side of the surgery was not appealing. *Does anyone care how ill I am becoming? Boy! Could I use a hug! Well, maybe a new pair of shoes for the trip too!*

The shoes were an easy fix. Penney found a perfect pair at the mall on her way home from the high school. The purchase got her in the mood for packing. When she got on the plane with Jack on Saturday, she was relaxed in her travel mode and sporting her new shoes. Penney was asleep when the plane took off, and she woke only to change planes. The layover in Beijing was long enough to allow the two of them to get a firsthand glimpse at the city's preparations for the Olympic Games and to try out one of the upscale restaurants at the new airport. Then on to the next plane.

Jack and Penney arrived late in Kuala Lumpur to discover their luggage was still in transit. Explaining their plight to the night clerks at the hotel, Penney and Jack were quickly presented with toiletries, pajamas, and a change of clothes for the next day—interestingly, all in their correct sizes.

Ever the consummate shopper, the very next morning Penney was up and dressed to go shopping shortly after Jack left for the day to attend his meetings. Penney wanted to acclimate herself to her surroundings on her own on this, her first day in Kuala Lumpur. Waving to the people at the reception desk, Penney headed for a café nearby, which she thought would be promising for a good cup of coffee, maybe even a latte. Her hopes answered, she sat down with a latte tasting faintly of toasted marshmallows and savored her first bite of a luscious chocolate pastry. *Ahhh, now I can get down to business.* She studied the map of downtown that she had picked up on the way to their room last night. Watching the women pass nearby, Penney was certain she could find a beautiful scarf, or two, or maybe three. The majority of women Penney observed wore scarves.

Following her breakfast, Penney quickly found that every store tempted her with gorgeous scarves. She, however, needed a particular size to fit her now–bald head. Searching for the right size, Penney was to learn that what she was actually looking for was a shawl.

As Penney lifted the navy scarf with purple and mustard-colored flowers dancing around the borders, a voice behind her said, "Uh, no. Let me show you."

Penney looked into the mirror to see a very attractive young woman hovering right behind her.

"It should be worn around the shoulders like this." The woman deftly threw a second scarf around her own shoulders while pointedly looking at Penney's own scarf tied at the side of her head.

Responding in self-defense, Penney simply said, "Cancer," blinking back the unbidden tears wanting to fall.

The woman now looked Penney over from head to toe. Slowly, the woman approached Penney and reached out to clasp Penney's free hand. Penney's other hand still clutched the navy scarf.

"Perhaps you would like to see a few other colors as well." The woman now looked gravely but earnestly at Penney.

Penney smiled and replied, "Yes, I would love to see what you might recommend." Penney took a deep breath and swiped at the corners of her eyes.

With that, Penney was shown colors and patterns she had never seen before—shades of intense fuchsia, sienna, and turquoise, spun with gold thread to further accent the extreme hues. Penney left with not only the navy scarf, but a few other stunning ones as well.

The rest of the day, Penney alternated between shopping and people-watching. She discovered that most Malay women wore bright colors. The ever-present gold thread made those colors pop from every angle. Many of the city's Indians also wore colorful sarongs. In addition, the Muslim women wore bright headscarves to do their shopping. The day was heady, with not only color, but beauty surrounding Penney.

When Penney returned to the hotel, she checked in with the concierge to learn what sights were must-sees. The concierge had several ideas and offered a guide to escort Penney around the city. Penney was soon to learn that her every whim on this trip was to be served. While Jack attended business meetings during the day, Penney immersed herself in the treasures of the city. The driver and the hotel's concierge arranged lunch reservations and tickets to wherever she wanted to go.

Penney visited the magnificent International Orchid Show one afternoon. Here she was dazzled by the number of orchids in every size and description. She found herself particularly enthralled by those plants flaunting tiny, delicate buds, their miniature cheeks preparing to explode into a kaleidoscope of color. Fragile, yes, but they were bursting with readiness to bring beauty into the world. Hovering over this extravaganza of flowery decadence were the famous Petronas Twin Towers, two glittery gems she relished from a distance that afternoon. The very next day, Penney toured this amazing architectural feat. Two bejeweled fingers rising up, up into the sky, the towers had been scaled by a Frenchman emulating Spiderman years before. The towers were not unfamiliar to Penney, but their immensity was daunting. They seemed to kiss the sun's rays, yet Penney knew they were constructed to protect visitors from the sun's damage. Actually built based on a simple design of Islamic geometric forms resembling stars, the shapes themselves represented the Islamic principles of "unity within unity, harmony, stability, and rationality." Penney took time to reflect when she reached level eighty-six, realizing that these very principles were what she wanted very much to maintain in her life. To think she had had to travel halfway around the world to achieve this clarity!

Later that evening, Penney dined on traditional Malaysian food in one of the many hotel restaurants. She was served grandly as she had come to expect. Following dinner, she sat back in an overstuffed chair to enjoy a fine glass of wine, silently reveling in all she had seen and done. The music was starting, and her feet were tapping to the beat. The lounge was filling, as it appeared the conference had let out. Suddenly, Jack loomed before her, his hand out, inviting her to dance. The dance floor was empty, but the two of them quickly filled the space with their dance moves. The band seemed to have every one of their favorite rock songs in their repertoire. Penney and Jack danced the entirety of each set. At the end of the evening, Jack smothered Penney with hugs and kisses. Many complimented the two of them on their dancing as they sat finishing their drinks. They returned to their room flushed with the thrill of the music, the dancing, and the joy of having this time together. This led to Penney falling asleep in Jack's arms, but not to intercourse. Penney accepted it as a baby step in the right direction.

VI

O n the other end of this rather surreal trip, Penney spent a personal day catching up with most of her integrative treatment practitioners. First stop was at her chiropractor's office to get all the kinks of traveling taken out. He was excited to hear about her travels, so this was a pleasant visit, as always. Next, Penney drove to the lab, where her blood work was done prior to her chemo treatment to make sure her blood cell counts could sustain a treatment. As usual, it took the phlebotomist three attempts to locate a viable vein in her right arm. There was even talk about using the veins in her foot if need be. A massage followed, so that helped to calm her a little. Vein-hunting was growing increasingly traumatic. The day ended with a session with her spiritual healer, Rita.

Rita's home seemed to always rest in a cloud of calm. When she opened her door to Penney, Penney could feel the weight beginning to lift from her shoulders. Rita asked about Penney's trip and the last couple of weeks and then zeroed in on Penney's blues.

"Penney, I have been conferring with Karishma and Cree. We all know this recent diagnosis is causing you stress. Can you talk to me about it?"

Penney took a long, slow, deep breath and began, "I am concerned that I wasn't fully recovered from my first round of treatment. The new stuff seems to be working, but the side effects are far greater than

I was told to expect. The fatigue can hit like a brick and from out of nowhere. And honestly, I am people-shy. They are backing away again, whether they know it or not. Now more than ever, I need hugs and hope, not hisses and hate. I can't do this alone—or should I say that I don't want to do this alone?—this time around. You talk about the message in all this, but I see it as dirty pool. It's impossible to hit the side pockets, let alone the ones right in front of me."

Rita had taken notes as Penney spoke. Her face was swathed in concern as she wrote. Penney was typically not this forthcoming with her, so she knew she had to respond strategically. "Let's take each of those one by one. You are right to look at your health and well-being. Nobody can take care of us quite like we ourselves can. How often are you seeing Karishma and Cree? I know they are working on your physical complaints."

"I see them each a couple of times a month, usually Cree before a treatment and Karishma after a treatment."

"How about if you do the Reiki with Cree a little more often?"

"Sure. I can do that."

"The people thing I understand, given your previous experiences. However, I believe you are going to have to work a few of them. Why not start with your good friend from your earlier job? You have shared that she always has a hug for you when the two of you get together. Jack sounds more involved this time around, so he needs to be in your people loop too."

"Okay. Okay. You're right. I'll talk to Amity. Jack, I think, is still a work in progress."

Rita nodded her head thoughtfully. "The message we are going to start working on right now. I'm going to take you on a journey where you are traveling side by side with your cancer and talking about the grand plan cancer has for you. Then we'll end with a little concert using the crystal singing bowls' tones to clear your mind. Let's get you up on the table in a more relaxed position."

Tone therapy was one of Penney's favorite healing methods. The journey prior to the crystal bowls' therapeutic vibrations found Penney visualizing a stroll into the universe alongside a serpent who reluctantly suggested she was destined to be a healer herself. Interesting, but the purpose still eluded Penney. After the journey and tone therapy, Rita recommended that Penney sit down across from her cancer and pursue further the conversation that she had begun with the serpent on the journey.

Penney returned home, driving into the setting sun and feeling somewhat restored. Rita had nourished her body, mind, and spirit. She wished she could hang onto this feeling for a long, long time.

She was still a little jet-lagged from her trip, so with the extra relaxation exercises from the day, she was able to sleep fairly well that night. The next morning, following her morning meditation and exercise routines, she gave Amity a call. Amity jumped at the chance to accompany Penney to her next chemo treatment. Penney sold her with the enticement that Amity could watch Penney spend tens of thousands of dollars without ever leaving the chemo room. Then, of course, there would be lunch and shopping after the chemo.

Penney put in a full day of work after talking to Amity. She worked with Jon and Sean on a few changes to the staff and student handbooks. Assisting her secretaries, Penney helped with the distribution of arriving teacher supplies to each teacher's classroom. She went over classroom furniture inventory with the head custodian. Meeting with the head football coach, she weighed the pros and cons of various fundraising options for the team. At the end of the day, Penney met with Frank to go over new teacher applications. She had not felt too badly during the day and drove to her lymphedema specialist appointment feeling relaxed. After a quiet dinner with Jack, she enjoyed another good night's sleep.

Amity arrived bright and early the next morning to drive Penney to Sirrah Glen. She gave Penney a long, tight hug before Penney could get a good look at her. Amity had dressed for the occasion, complete with hot pink jeans color-coordinated with the pink highlights in her blond hair. The two of them together were a study in pinks. The drive to Sirrah Glen seemed to go quickly as the two women chatted about educational issues large and small.

Arriving at Dr. Salvatore's office, Tess was delighted to meet Amity. Tess gushed over their pink outfits. For her part, Amity took charge of the infusion situation immediately. Once ensconced in the chemo room, Amity kept right on top of the chemo procedures. As soon as one bag of medication was emptied, Amity was ringing the bell for Tess to come and get Penney started on the next step. They talked and laughed all day, and each bought too many pairs of shoes at the end of the day. Having thanked Amity for being a darn good friend, Penney blew her kisses as Amity pulled away from Penney's home. It had been a good day.

The rest of the week Penney kept pretty low-key, as the anticipated side effects did indeed manifest: body and scalp rash, nosebleeds, uneasy abdominal area, chills, aches all over her body, periods of feeling down, and now dizziness added to the list. Penney called Dr. Salvatore's office right away about the dizziness and got an immediate response. That office was impressive. While she was currently crashing at night, Penney was nevertheless exhausted for several days after the treatment. This was even with extra hours of sleep and a visit to Karishma, who was treating her fatigue with both acupuncture and Chinese herbs. As always, Penney discovered a new fount of energy after her visit to Karishma, but these bursts of energy were fading faster and faster following each treatment.

When Penney ventured to the spa later in the week, the entire spa crew met her at the door with hugs. They were eager to inform her that they had arranged to close the spa on the upcoming Wednesday so that they could take her to her next chemo treatment and then to visit a spa near Sirrah Glen owned by a friend of theirs. There, they were treating her to a spa treatment of her choice. This caught Penney completely off guard and brought on a flood of joyful tears. All she could get out was a "Thank you!"

The "spa girls" did not disappoint. They picked Penney up in a luxurious van that they had outfitted with pillows encased in pink silk pillowcases, lavender eye pillows, and purple merino throws. They had her icy-cold water in an ice chest for her. Throughout the entire day, Penney had only to ask and she got it. They took turns massaging her during the actual chemo treatment. This was interrupted, however, when Dr. Salvatore unexpectedly showed up.

After walking Penney back to her office, Dr. Salvatore explained that when she had seen Penney's name on the patient list for today, she had arranged to slip away from the hospital and come see Penney. She had been looking some more at Penney's options. Breast conservation, she had concluded, should really not be on the table. She felt Penney was going to need a mastectomy. She gave Penney the names of two surgeons whom she knew could handle the scope of the surgery Penney would need. Dr. Salvatore also wanted Penney to come in for treatment once a week now until the surgery plans were solidified. They would be stopping the steroids and Aloxi after today's treatment, as Dr. Salvatore believed they were causing more issues than they were solving. Penney also learned Dr. Salvatore had had a call from Dr. Anthony to check on Penney and to say he was going on sabbatical. Having no questions for Dr. Salvatore, Penney thanked her for coming to see her and returned to her chemo room. Penney was pleased things were moving forward, but not entirely happy with where they were moving.

The girls made her comfortable once again. Penney acted as if nothing out of the ordinary had happened, but she was suddenly really missing Jack's presence and his counsel. When they stopped at the girls' friend's spa on the way home, Penney had a few moments all to herself. A tear wound its way down her cheek as she tried to gather her thoughts. This day with the girls was fun and relaxing, but she unmistakably knew she was not heading to a fun and relaxing new road ahead. At the end of the day, the girls gave her a group hug and showered her with smiles and well-wishes. And then they were off.

When Penney went over Dr. Salvatore's visit with Jack, he seemed to take the information in stride. "So, Penney, it is the next step. You have been certain all along that the surgery was going to be pretty major. Let's check out those surgeons Dr. Salvatore has recommended. We'll go from there. We are going to beat this this time."

"You're right. I'm just so tired, and I don't want to keep getting more compromised healthwise. Jack, I want to be well again." Penney slumped to the chair and let her head fall forward.

"And you will be, Penney. Together we'll get through this, I promise." Jack knelt in front of Penney and lifted her chin in his hand.

Penney blinked back tears. Jack stood her up and took her in his arms. He didn't let go for a long time.

Freshmen orientation was Monday. Penney made it through many uncomfortable looks from parents, smiling all the while. When she spoke to the large group, though, there was little doubt in anyone's mind that she was very much in charge. Penney popped into each small group tour to give a more personalized welcome as each group was guided by a senior to tour the high school. By the end of the morning, she had won over more hearts. Jon and Sean high-fived one another in the background, saying, "That's our Mrs. D!"

Wednesday was there before she knew it, and she and Jack made the trip to Sirrah Glen. The treatment went much faster with no pre-meds to be administered. Jack and Penney were packing up almost as soon as they had unpacked, it seemed. They had lunch at an Italian restaurant where they were now recognized and doted upon.

The next week went fairly smoothly, including minimal side effects. Penney had moments of feeling like her old self. Not delusional, though, she knew chemo was just around the corner yet again. To top it off, the day Penney had been dreading since her treatment started now reared its ugly head.

Penney had come home from work and ran up the stairs to check on Jack. He looked up from his computer and casually informed Penney, "I have a very important conference call tomorrow, so I can't take you to Sirrah Glen."

Penney peered at him in disbelief. *How is this "getting through this together"?*

"You can't take the call in the chemo room?" Penney asked with wonder in her voice.

"Actually, Penney, this cancer is eating into my time and my work, a lot. The answer is no. I have to give this particular discussion my undivided attention. You were fine after last week's treatment. If you have to stop on the way home, give me a call." Jack pulled back from his desk and crossed his arms across his chest.

"Okay, then. I'll be fine." Penney walked away so that her quivering chin and moistened eyes could not be seen. She didn't know quite what to make of that little exchange, but she did know enough not to want to pursue it. Penney could not shake the uncanny feeling that a serpent was slowly coiling itself up her leg.

Jack returned to his work as she passed through his office door.

Penney made the trip down to Sirrah Glen alone but without incident. Once she was there, however, her veins just would not cooperate. Tess had to bring in another nurse to find a vein that could be used. Penney had seen this nurse from afar. She was big-boned, with rather harsh facial features. Penney knew she was not a smiler, which immediately set her apart from the rest of the team. Her approach seemed to be matter-of-fact, with little conversation as she worked with patients.

This nurse, introduced as Liza, proceeded to tell Penney her veins were shot. Once she found a vein that could be used, Liza proceeded to give Penney a piece of her own thoughts. She didn't know or understand why Penney did not have a port, but she needed to get one before her treatment next week, or they would very likely have to suspend further treatments. Liza was openly hostile and disgusted with Penney. Tess tried to make things better, but Penney was rattled. Jack called during her actual treatment to check on her. Penney informed him she was fine and would be home later.

Following her treatment, Penney drove straight to Dr. Anthony's old office, hoping to speak with his surgical partner, Dr. Gallagher. Appearing quite distraught, she was not kept waiting long. Dr. Gallagher himself brought her back to his office. His tall, athletic frame loomed over Penney's muscled but slight build.

"We have been wondering how you were doing. You know that Dr. Anthony is on sabbatical?" Dr. Gallagher gave her his full attention, sensing her frustration.

"Yes, I had heard that. I had an issue today at chemo, and I would like to hear your thoughts on the matter." Penney was flushed and a little breathless.

"Okay. Tell me what's going on." Dr. Gallagher sat forward in his chair, scanning Penney's drawn face.

Penney explained where she was at with her current treatment and what was on the horizon. "So, what do you think? I drove straight here, not even certain why or if I would be seen."

"Penney, the insertion of a medi-port is pretty straightforward. It does require going to the operating room and being given a local anesthetic. While there are benefits to having a medi-port for chemo infusion, let me see if I can voice some of your hesitation."

"Okay. I apologize for being so disordered. Normally, I am well-rehearsed, but this has really upset me."

"Well, some of your distress, I think, is understandable. First off, your immune system is under stress with the low blood cell count you report. It is further compromised by the bleeding due to the Avastin. That is not optimal for even a minor surgery. Secondly, the surgery coming up which you described involves the chest wall area where I would prefer placing a port. This could complicate your upcoming surgery, so the port very likely would have to be removed. Once it is removed, that same vein cannot be used for a new port. I have to tell you I don't believe this is an optimal time for placing a port. I'll do whatever you ask here, Penney, but there is some added risk for you."

"So where would you recommend they access a vein for the next few weeks?" Penney was still wild-eyed and clearly distressed.

"Tell them to use the crease. And, Penney, know we're here for you if you need us."

They rose together and shook hands, and Penney went on her way. She couldn't help but wonder why she had not been sent to Dr. Gallagher initially. He actually communicated with her.

Jack met her at the door as she exited her car. Penney informed him she was tired and did indeed fall immediately asleep for a couple of hours as soon as her head touched the pillow.

The next few days, including the weekend, were uneventful: projects at work, chores around the house. Monday, the teachers returned to prepare their classrooms for the new school year. Over the next two days, Penney met with the full faculty, with the department chairs, and with individual teachers. She knew better than to expect them to ask how she was, but she was disappointed nonetheless when not even a few broached the topic. Again, there was the stealthy assessment of her physical person as she spoke. Penney had done this little romp before, and she knew it was best to keep moving along. Through the grapevine, she would learn how she was doing. It was typically way off the mark and could be humorous.

Penney did see Cree at the end of the day on Monday after that very full day at the high school. As usual, Penney floated out of the session at peace with herself and feeling energized. The drive to Dr. Salvatore's office on Wednesday unsettled her reverie a little as she anticipated a showdown with Liza.

Tess met Penney in the waiting room, asked after Jack but noticed the flicker of pain in Penney's eyes, and moved on to ask how Penney's veins were doing. Penney explained about using the crease. Tess tried not to look surprised and suggested they move on to the chemo suite, where hot cloths were placed up and down Penney's right arm to help coax her veins along. Penney focused all her energy into this endeavor. It worked! The entire treatment went quickly and smoothly. Penney did not even catch a glimpse of Liza. She took herself out to lunch and then did a little shopping. Her smile was back. She got a huge latte to help keep her focused on the ride home.

Jack prepared some of her favorite things for dinner: salmon, sweet potatoes, and brussels sprouts. Penney declared the meal delicious and then went off to bed by herself, where she slept soundly through the night. Jack did not come to bed until quite some time later. He had much to ponder.

The next day, Penney saw Karishma, who treated her for her ongoing abdominal complaints, depleted energy reservoirs, and related meridians. Karishma looked Penney over as she removed the needles at the end of the session. From long association, she knew

Penney was working too hard in order to keep all her irons in the fire. The chemo was taking its toll, and Penney, she knew all too well, would not be throwing in the towel.

"Penney, if I might make one suggestion, it would be that you take a half day for yourself midweek."

"Wednesday is my chemo day, so it is pretty much a wash anyway."

"Is Jack still traveling down with you?"

"No, not since they stopped the pre-meds. He thinks I'm fine."

"And are you fine?"

"Even I will admit that I am tired. This cancer stuff is hard work."

The two women looked squarely at one another.

"A short power nap daily would help."

"Okay. I am trying. Right now, I need to get the students back to the high school. I need to feed off their energy."

"That, I know, is next week, so, good. Just take it easy, please."

The two women hugged and wished each other peace in the weeks to come.

Taking advantage of the long Labor Day weekend, Penney kept her promise to Karishma and did get in a nap each day. Typically, Penney and Jack would have been in Manhattan for this weekend, but with Penney's trip to Greece not too far off, they opted to stay home. For their anniversary that weekend, Jack took Penney to a very special local restaurant and presented her with an exquisite pair of diamond and sapphire earrings. She was speechless and reached for Jack's hand across the table.

As they studied one another, Jack spoke. "Penney, I do love you, more than you will ever know."

In her mind's eye, Penney could see the rays of the sun bringing the day to Paris while darkening the intimacy she had so enjoyed. She knew these words. She had heard them before. Penney searched Jack's face with tears in her eyes and whispered, "I know, Jack, I know." The evening ended with hugs and kisses and a final champagne toast before they tucked themselves in for the night. Penney tossed and turned while Jack slept soundly.

The first day of school arrived. Penney made it through the day proud and happy, greeting each of her twelve hundred students as they came in the main entrance. The students were seeing the totally completed renovation project for the first time in most cases. They gushed over the striking use of the school colors in the entrance area, the new gym, the library, and the cafeteria, which had turned into a full-fledged food court. Their response to Penney wearing her scarf again was unconditional respect. Several cocked their heads, gave her a thumbs-up, and firmly asserted, "You give it an even better fight this time, Mrs. Divan!" That and the many hugs and good wishes other students gave her made Penney renew her resolve to beat this monstrous disease.

The end of the first week of school marked the beginning of the high school's football season. On that warm Friday night, Penney and Jack helped cheer the young men on to victory. The next afternoon, Penney and Jack did the same for the boys' soccer team. Penney most certainly appeared to rally for her students.

Penney caught Jack looking at her wistfully while she visited with parents at the soccer match. She wished Jack wouldn't worry so much. Jack winked at her as he continued his assessment of the woman he loved. He was growing increasingly aware of the darkening shadows under Penney's eyes, her shoulders bent from fatigue, and the ever-ready tissue balled up in her finger tips should another nosebleed begin. Jack's thoughts took over. *How does she do this? I couldn't.* She was haunted, he knew, but look at her. She was full of strength and beauty! He was beginning to understand why some people found her intimidating. Following the soccer match, Jack walked out to the car with Penney, hoping more than ever this would all end soon. Penney cast a quick sideways glance at Jack, wondering where his thoughts had been while his gaze followed her at the match. She knew they both had to just keep moving along with all this.

Before making the next trip to Sirrah Glen, Penney and Jack sat down to carefully appraise the surgeons Dr. Salvatore was recommending to perform Penney's surgery. Both were well qualified, but one got high praise from Nell and a few of Nell's patients. Completing their inquiries with an online investigation, they concluded that a visit to Dr. Saks was in their future. When Wednesday arrived, Penney once again made the all-too-familiar trip to Sirrah Glen on her own. Though she did not entirely understand why, Penney was accepting that for whatever reason, Jack was no longer participating in her chemo treatments. He had announced he would be accompanying her to meet Dr. Saks when that visit was set up. Penney knew she would need him then.

Dr. Salvatore met Penney in the waiting area when Penney checked in. Together they went to Dr. Salvatore's office to briefly discuss Penney and Jack's decision. Dr. Salvatore escorted Penney to the chemotherapy suite and went back to her office to phone Dr. Saks. By the time Penney had finished her treatment, Dr. Salvatore was back to inform Penney that she had reviewed Penney's case with Dr. Saks. He was looking forward to meeting Penney on Tuesday after her chemo treatment. Penney's treatment had been moved up a day to accommodate Penney, who needed to be at the high school all day and through the evening on Wednesday for the dedication activities for the new building. Penney had all her bases covered now. She left Dr. Salvatore's office that day fully prepared to march into this next step of her cancer care with hope for a more lasting resolution and for a healthier future.

VII

Both Penney and Jack awakened Tuesday with great expectations. The air was still warm and allowed them to drive to Sirrah Glen with the top down. They arrived rosy-cheeked and in good spirits. Dr. Salvatore met with them after Penney had completed her treatment. Dr. Salvatore was excited about the tumor softening and shrinking, and she shared great hope for Penney's outcome. She also promised to check in with Penney regularly and reassured the two of them that Penney would be in good hands with Dr. Saks and his team.

The drive to Dr. Saks' office was quick, only about fifteen minutes away from Dr. Salvatore's office. Jack scanned for a seat in the luxuriously furnished waiting area while Penney checked in. Penney watched Jack wend his way through the maze of furniture and faces to settle in a corner. She marveled at how many people were in the waiting area at such a late hour. Once through the check-in process, Penney walked over and sat beside Jack, her arms full of forms to fill out As she moved through form after form, a tall, gangly young woman sat down beside her. Her pin said she was an RN.

"Hi! I'm Dana. Dr. Saks would like you to have a few tests while you are waiting. I'm going to take you over to radiology to get you started on an MRI, a mammogram, and an ultrasound." Her smile filled her round face, not unlike the yellow smiley faces decorating the space above the check-in desk.

"I'm Penney." Penney's eyes were beginning to narrow, and she could feel the vein in her temple starting to throb. "I have had all these tests very recently. I can tell you what they will show. Besides, you should have copies of the reports from all my previous testing."

"Ah, well, we need to have very current results. So just come with me…" Dana stood.

"I don't understand. These aren't necessary. I am here to meet with Dr. Saks to talk about surgery." Penney looked up at Dana, undeniably confused and growing frantic rapidly.

Dana sat down again. Penney, now visibly upset, was shaking her head no while she watched Dana's smile freeze.

Dana firmly repeated her request. "You need to do these tests."

Penney stared at Jack, who shrugged in return. He was engrossed in an e-mail on his computer.

Penney stood, shook off the chill running up and down her spine, and followed Dana through one of several doors opening into the waiting area. Penney was introduced to a technician named Celia, a short, stout brunette. Celia took Penney to the changing area, where the infamous gown awaited her. There was a cuddly robe to wear over it, especially good since it was chilly in this part of the suite. Celia also presented Penney with another pile of paperwork to complete. Penney took one look at the paperwork, saw it was the exact same set she had just filled in, and refused to repeat the drill. Celia tried valiantly to convince Penney that radiology was separate from Dr. Saks' office, and consequently they had to have Penney complete the information for them. Penney stood her ground. The two divisions did, after all, share the same computer programs, Penney was quite certain. They could always copy the forms as well.

Penney went through each test feeling like she had become a cog in a machine. Over an hour later, she was spat back out into the waiting area, robe and all. Jack was pacing, wondering where she had gone for so long. When she explained, he just shook his head. Before Penney could get comfortable, though, Dana popped up to take the two of them to meet with Dr. Saks. As the two of them waited in the exam room, Jack tried to reassure Penney that these people were just doing their jobs.

A flurry of activity and hushed conversation outside the exam room door brought their attention to the curtain hanging in front of the door. A knock on the door followed by "Hello" brought Dr. Saks into the room. He was tall and lanky with curly, chestnut-colored hair and brilliant blue eyes. Under his lab coat, he wore dress slacks, a striped tie, and loafers. As he shook Penney's and Jack's hands, he dryly announced, "You know, metaplastic carcinoma does not have a very good prognosis."

Dr. Saks was clearly not expecting the crestfallen look overtaking Penney's face, nor the despair Jack tried to cover up as he reached for Penney's hand. Dr. Saks' face was overcome with dismay.

"We've heard this before, Dr. Saks. You have to know you have one spirited woman in front of you who refuses to succumb to those odds." Jack squeezed Penney's hand, and she returned the squeeze.

"I have come here to fight, so please do not give in before we begin." Penney stared defiantly at Dr. Saks.

"Well, I think we do need to be realistic. Let's have a look at you, though, Penney. I want to check out some things that I didn't find entirely clear among the test results." Dr. Saks appeared lost in his thoughts for a moment.

Fighting back tears, Penney climbed up on the exam table. She helped to enlighten Dr. Saks as to where the tumor extended. Pulling in an ultrasound machine, Dr. Saks clearly identified what Penney was talking about. The tumor had surely infiltrated the pectoralis muscles. Still deep in thought, Dr. Saks discussed not only the necessity for a mastectomy, but also a radical mastectomy, removing the breast and the pectoralis muscles, as well as some contaminated skin from the previous surgery.

Penney was white as a sheet but managed to ask about reconstruction, the option for a double mastectomy, and what such a surgery would mean for her routines. Jack asked dozens of questions, ending with, "And what if she doesn't go through with this ugly scenario?"

"It would bring us back to my initial, and much too hasty, conclusion. Penney and Jack, this is undeniably serious. We can do it together, though. You have asked good questions. I would like to confer with Dr. Salvatore again. I am also going to set you up with plastic surgery for a consultation. And I would like a more current PET/CT scan. The surgery should be fairly soon, so I do not want you doing any more chemotherapy, and especially Avastin, at this juncture. I also understand from Dr. Salvatore, Penney, that you have a trip coming up. You need to enjoy this trip first. We'll find a date for the scan after you return." Dr. Salvatore looked at both Penney and Jack. It had been quite a while since he had met such an astute couple. He wanted to work with them. Should he tell them he had never done a radical mastectomy? No, he would prepare. "So, do either of you have any more questions?"

Jack and Penney looked at one another and shook their heads to indicate they had no more questions.

"All right. If questions do come up, call my office or Dana. We will get back to you. Safe travels!" He waved to them on his way out.

Penney turned to Jack and said, "I don't think I like him."

"Penney, he has a plan. I'm not saying I do like him, but I don't not like him either. Let's get out of here and find some dinner."

Penney checked out with the lone receptionist still in the office. The large waiting room was completely empty, making the three of them appear lost in the vast space. Once outside, Penney looked up to note that the sky was beginning to play host to the stars. The full moon was already watching over them as they walked to their car at the far end of the parking lot. Penney immediately thought Rita would say the moon and the stars were omens, positive omens. Though all the hope she had built up with Dr. Salvatore had been dashed in a single sentence, Penney knew she must continue to place one foot in front of the other and move forward. She took three long, deep breaths and closed her eyes. She visualized herself happy, healthy, and with hair! She smiled. She could do this! Jack had the car started and was ready to go.

The ultimate distraction awaited her the next day, the long-anticipated day for the building dedication of the completed renovation project. Penney met Frank in her office at seven AM, and the festivities immediately began to unfold. A VIP breakfast was hosted by Penney in her private conference room. These guests included a state congressman, the mayor, the school board president, and the president and vice president of the student council, along with Frank, Penney, Jon, and Sean. Serving a hot breakfast prepared by her students in the culinary arts program at the nearby vocational/technical school, Penney gloated over her students while gushing about the new café and kitchen in the high school. When it was time to move to the theater for the formal dedication ceremony, Penney led the dignitaries through the sparkling blue-and-green hallways. Penney herself wore the school colors. She was dressed in a brilliant blue sheath and a relaxed emerald-green blazer with coordinated accessories. Her Italian silk scarf picked up both colors in a contemporary pattern with black and white mixed in.

The senior class and the local media joined Penney's entourage in the theater. The speakers were each entertaining, from the designer of the building to the school board president to Frank. When it came time for the state congressman to speak, he praised Penney's vision for the project from beginning to end. Penney thanked everyone, most especially the staff and the students, who had made education happen in spite of the chaos surrounding them during the project.

The festivities continued throughout the day and into the evening, as tours for the community took over after the school day ended. Penney put in a very busy fourteen-hour day. She was a little tired, she had to admit, but as she stood in the main entrance area bidding a good evening to the final people vacating the building, she smiled with pride. This was a huge accomplishment, and she felt like she could achieve just about anything.

First, though, Penney would take a break. She was going to Greece. Jack put her on the plane on Friday, not without a little trepidation. He knew she was doing better lately, but this trip involved changing planes three times before she arrived in the tiny Greek village she was headed to. She wouldn't even meet up with Ginger until the last leg. Jack found himself wondering once again where she found the strength to keep moving on. Penney waved to him from the steps of the commuter plane. Her brightly colored scarf swirled around her right shoulder in the wind. Dressed in jeans, turtleneck, and boots, Penney appeared healthy from a distance. She was off to have fun. Jack cracked a smile, quashing his concern.

Penney made all of her connections, used a little French to ask for directions to her gate in Zurich, and hugged Ginger for an extra-long time when she found her at the airport in Dusseldorf. They called Jack, relieving him of some of his tension. Next, they called Ken, who wished the two of them a great vacation. And then, it was time for the mother-daughter holiday to begin.

When they arrived in Preveza late at night, they found that the one-room air terminal was empty. While Ginger collected their luggage, Penney walked outside to find a cab. The night was pitch black, with only scattered stars peeking through the clouds to light her way. Penney thought she saw a few cars parked a ways down the road. One, she discovered, actually looked like a cab, and its driver was sound asleep behind the wheel. She lightly tapped on the window, startling the man out of his sleep. He rolled down his window, and Penney explained what resort they needed to find.

"Sure. I have been waiting for you. There are two of you, no?" He spoke in near-perfect English.

Surprised, Penney replied, "Yes!"

"Get in. I will take you back to the terminal, so we can get all your things. The place you are staying is about forty minutes away."

The three of them packed their belongings into the trunk. Away they went in the night over more dirt roads, through fields and pastures, and ending up on a recently paved road leading to the resort. Penney thanked the cab driver and paid him, including a generous tip. He responded with a wide, warm smile and a wave. As he pulled away, he announced, "See you tomorrow!"

Penney and Ginger both looked at one another, laughed, and went into the reception area, where lights glittered. There, a young woman behind the desk greeted them, also in perfect English, and presented each of them with a glass of champagne. She too indicated she had been expecting them. They wound their way to their two-bedroom condo, gave each other quick good night hugs, and fell immediately asleep in their bedrooms.

Penney woke to find her room flooded with sunshine. She quietly moved to the curtains to pull them aside for the sun in all its glory to shower the entire room. What she saw took her breath away. Her room opened onto a private veranda overlooking the well-laid-out resort, its beautifully appointed grounds brilliant with the showy splendor of dizzying arrays of colorful flowers in every direction, the surrounding manicured fields, and the very aqua-blue waters of the Ionian Sea. Ginger's room also opened up to this spacious veranda.

Penney rapped on Ginger's door, saying, "Ginger, get up! Get up! You are not going to believe this!"

When Ginger opened her door, her jaw dropped too. "Cool! I'll go get coffee. You stay right here and enjoy the view."

Penney pulled a bistro set away from the wall and over to the railing. Then she sat, taking it all in. Penney's thoughts were many. *I can relax and just be myself here amidst all this beauty. Ahhh! Ten days to do, or not do, whatever I want. This is why I travel. It is the quintessential escape and renewal for me. Life is good, and I will endure.* Penney blinked several times in order to refresh her sheer delight in ingesting the view.

Ginger returned with two individual coffee plungers. They leisurely enjoyed their coffee while basking in the beauty, waving to others walking the resort grounds, and planning their week.

Long walks during the days ahead enabled them to visit the quaint neighboring villages, old unmarked ruins, verdant farmlands, vast olive groves, and winding country roads leading them into the hillsides. Sure enough, each evening their taxi driver from the airport appeared to take them to dinner in Preveza, where the choices of both restaurants and menu items were always varied and tempting. They dined on open terraces sampling traditional *tzatziki, tiropitakia, stifado,* and *yaourtopita,* as well as classic *spanakopita, papoutsakia,* and *souvlaki.* The wine was always drawn from an unlabeled cask. All nights were declared delightful and yummy!

A typical adventure would lead them far into the rustic countryside. Early in the week, Penney and Ginger decided to follow the signs that they hoped would take them to a well-advertised restaurant. As the path narrowed, the villas on either side of the path grew larger and more stately.

"It is starting to look like something I would imagine out of one of those books that talks about moving into the European countryside and revitalizing an older estate," observed Penney as the two of them moved up the hill.

The path was now lined with neatly planted olive trees. Every once in a while, a gate would beckon to Penney and Ginger to take a peek. They would gaze upon beautifully restored homes surrounded by geometrically perfect plantings of green foliage and fall blooms.

"You know, Mom, you're right. It's almost like a movie set."

They continued on their hike, enjoying the combination of rusticity and gentle refinement on either side of them. At the top of the hill rose an old country farmhouse. Outside were tables and chairs encircling a firepit. A young woman worked among the tables laying out linens and cutlery.

Together, Penney and Ginger declared, "I think we've found it!" as the young woman beckoned for them to come forward.

"We don't often get people up here during the day. Come, come, come. Have a coffee with us."

The young woman led them inside, where an older woman stood at the kitchen bar chopping vegetables feverishly. The older woman was not as slim as the younger woman, but the flawless olive-toned skin, the wild profusion of ringlets framing her face, and that welcoming sparkle in her eyes suggested they were related.

"Look, Mama! Two tourists, and I don't think they are British!"

Penney and Ginger laughed, introducing themselves as very American.

"Sit, please. You must have coffee with us."

The coffee plungers came out. The conversation bubbled. The topics moved from mother–daughter relationships to travel to cooking. The laughter flowed. Penney and Ginger promised to return for dinner when Mama, with a discerning eye, observed that Penney could use a little fattening up.

Their taxi driver that evening heartily approved of their dinner destination, describing the meal they would be enjoying. When the taxi pulled up in front of the old farmhouse, Penney recognized most of the diners as guests at their resort, all of whom were indeed British.

Exiting the cab, Penney and Ginger were immediately greeted with, "You came back! You are here! Let me take you to a special table!"

Special it was! Mama placed them at a table for two outside that also had a commanding view of the kitchen on the inside. Mama served each course herself, describing its preparation and possible variations on each recipe.

They began with vegetable *dolmades* with yogurt garlic sauce, followed by ouzo-cured salmon with fennel and dill. Next, they were treated to a *hortopita*, a wild greens pie. Then the appetizer arrived: seared sea scallops with Greek fava and red onion, tomato, and caper stew. The salad course was an octopus salad with grilled peppers, tomatoes, and baby greens. For the main course, grilled lamb chops with Ionian garlic sauce, which Mama served with a twinkle in her eye. Their wine glasses were never left empty. At this point in the meal, Penney and Ginger were more than satisfied, but they surely had to try the dessert, Mama was quick to assure them. Mama proudly carried out the baked quince with Samos syrup.

"You are lucky! This is the first quince of the season. It will bring you much luck, health, and happiness!"

"Amen to that!" pronounced Penney while she took a spoonful of the luscious fruit dessert.

Ginger pulled back from the table, grinning from ear to ear. "You know, Mom, this is quite a meal. The fact that we are being treated like royalty is not going unnoticed either."

Penney looked around and did detect an air of *"Who are they?"* She laughed. "Why, Ginger, we're just the cook's and the owner's coffee-drinking buddies!"

Their smiles carried all the way through their hugs goodbye. Penney felt loved. She knew that was all she needed for the moment.

Penney and Ginger hired their cab driver mid-week to take them over to the next island to shop and to eat some more. There they sampled fish caught from the sea that morning and bought artisan-designed jewelry from the artists themselves. Toward the end of the week, they joined several other vacationers on a sailboat to visit a few of the more outlying islands. It rained all day, making vacating the sailboat to go ashore most often impossible, but no one cared. They were all having too much fun getting to know one another. Occasionally, during the week, someone would ask Penney how she was feeling, to which she happily replied, "I am doing well today. Thank you for asking."

At the end of the week, Penney and Ginger boarded a plane to fly to Athens for a few days. From their hotel there, they could view the Parthenon lit up at night. What a spectacular marvel! Its classic Greek architecture dominated the night sky. This also put them within easy walking distance of many of the prominent sites. The Acropolis itself commanded the city from its hilltop trajectory, with the Parthenon just one of its many glorious features. Penney became enamored with the lore surrounding the Temple of Olympian Zeus. Long since fallen into ruin, the Temple still stands, if only fifteen columns. Penney viewed it as a testimony to endurance. A large part of the world's population, it seemed, had also decided to visit Athens during these few days. The streets were teeming with people, with life. Penney loved it!

Their last afternoon, while gorging on chocolate baklava and Greek coffee at a sidewalk café, Ginger did ask, "Mom, how are you really? You seem so full of life, but well, how are you? I'm worried."

"Ginger, I'm scared, but I won't give up. And, no, I do not agree that I am as close to death as many would like me to believe. What you see before you is how I am, living with a chronic disease. Life moves forward. So shall you and I. Don't worry quite so much. Now, where shall we eat tonight?" They both flashed one another that easy Divan smile. Their last meal in Athens was magnificent—though they both agreed nothing could compare with Mama's meal!

In the pre-dawn hours of the next morning, Penney brushed a kiss on her sleeping daughter's forehead and walked back into the world she had left behind for a short while. The taxi driver who picked her up from the hotel was very eager to engage her in conversation. He was also well traveled, and the trip to the airport went quickly as the two of them shared memories of places they had been. They agreed that there were still many more places to see. All they needed was time.

The next day, Jack watched her descend from the commuter plane he had recently watched her fly away in. She was returning with a healthy tan and her ever-ready smile, looking much more rested. *That's my girl!* he thought.

Penney fell right back into her routines, with acupuncture, a visit to Rita, and school activities rounding out her calendar. Only two evenings after she returned home, Penney hosted a back-to-school night program at the high school. She visited classrooms alongside the parents and participated in the activities that the teachers had planned. Later in the week, she attended a volleyball game accompanied by Jon and Sean. On Friday, she and Jack watched the football team win a rousing victory.

The PET/CT scan occurred at the end of the following week. This brought her to the much-anticipated consultation visit with the plastic surgeon and the sarcoma surgeon. Penney and Jack met with Dr. Saks beforehand to review the results of the scan. Nothing new. Penney still had the worrisome tumor in a precarious location. Dr. Saks suggested that reconstruction might best be delayed, but Penney was holding firm. Off Penney and Jack went to meet with Dr. Svensen and Dr. Andersen.

The check-in was quick. Penney and Jack were ushered in to an exam room, where they waited for only a brief time. The room was uninspired, done in tones of beige: beige walls, beige cabinets, beige furnishings.

The door to the exam room opened. Two Adonis-like figures filled the doorway. Each man was tanned and toned, dressed in a strikingly white lab coat. They both had heads of curly, sun-bleached blond hair accented by aquamarine eyes gazing from unlined faces. The one in front, however, overshadowed the other man in stature and sheer presence.

His booming voice announced, "Mrs. Divan, you may not have immediate reconstruction. You most likely will not live much more than a year, if that. Dr. Andersen here agrees." (Dr. Andersen was nodding his head up and down.) "It is too time-consuming, and your prognosis is very, very poor. You should never have been referred here. Good day."

As the two men turned to leave, Jack rose from his chair to say, "Wait just a minute. Penney does have a say in this. I think you need to hear us out."

"No, I don't. Dr. Andersen is in agreement with me." (Dr. Andersen was now feverishly shaking his head up and down. Penney thought he might be starting to pant.) "It would be wrong for us to entertain such a procedure for her." He scrutinized Penney from head to toe, shaking his own head in obvious disgust. His features were more pronounced. He was clearly growing angry, as his eyes narrowed. Dr. Andersen kept bobbing his head up and down.

Penney had sat quietly, her head down. As she sat up straighter, she looked carefully at both surgeons, and then asked, "Why exactly is it that we cannot at least discuss my options? Why do I not have the opportunity to be whole and beautiful like any other woman?"

Dr. Svensen took one step toward her and started plucking at her belly. "You have no tissue, even. And look at this breast! It's deformed. You cannot ask to be beautiful. You are dying. Dying!" He laced his fingers together in front of his chest.

Penney murmured in a hushed voice, "Perhaps I need another opinion." Her eyes were piercing as she focused on Dr. Svensen's face. "Good day to you, then!"

"No one will touch your case!" he shouted. With that, he stormed out of the room with Dr. Andersen following in his shadow, that head of his still wobbling on his neck.

Penney and Jack looked long and hard at one another. Jack spoke first.

"Okay. I don't like these guys, Penney."

"Jack, why is it that cancer brings out the worst in so many people? I feel defiled and debased. I'll show that creepy bully! I will be beautiful!"

Jack pulled Penney to him and hugged her tenderly. "Penney, you are beautiful, and in so many ways. Let me talk to Dr. Saks and sort this out."

"I love you, Jack, but I am doing this my way, you know."

"Oh, I know, Penney. I know."

"And I am not done living."

"I know that too." He kissed her and turned her toward the dressing area in the room.

Penney quickly put herself back together. They both were anxious to get away from this particular office.

Jack talked to Dr. Saks the very next day. Dr. Svensen had already spoken with Dr. Saks, relaying his firm conviction that Penney and Jack were two crazy people whom he would never work with. Jack was equally adamant that Penney was not to be seen by Dr. Svensen at any time for any reason. He was also very clear that Penney's request for immediate reconstruction would be honored. Dr. Saks was profusely apologetic and assured Jack he would do everything possible to get Penney another consult. Within the hour, Penney received a call from another plastic surgeon's office to set up a date and time for a new consultation.

That accomplished, Penney and Jack went back to their respective jobs and lives. Penney worked hard during the day, visiting classrooms to do teacher observations when not meeting with staff members, students, and parents. To rev up her energy and her spirit, Penney had appointments at the spa, as well as with Rita, Karishma, and Cree. As for Jack, he left for a two-week business trip to Asia.

This would mean Penney would attend her next plastic surgery consultation on her own. Here, she was ushered into a room done in blues and whites, gauze tulle used to create a dust ruffle for the exam table and a cover for shelves holding supplies. It was very cozy and comfortable for an exam room.

Penney was quickly joined by Dr. Tirion. He was of medium height and medium build, with dark brown hair cut close to his head. He wore khakis and a short-sleeved sport shirt under an open lab coat. He was young and relaxed, immediately sitting down in the chair beside Penney. He had reviewed her case, and she learned he had attended a medical, multidisciplinary conference with Dr. Saks that morning where her case had been discussed. All there had agreed that immediate reconstruction could certainly be pursued.

Penney's happiness over this news was difficult to contain. She smiled widely, shook Dr. Tirion's hand, and softly offered, "Thank you!"

When she got to her car, she did a little merengue dance, hoping not to draw anyone's attention. She looked up to the sky and watched the clouds drift by. *Yes, there is hope in the universe, after all.*

Penney had three weeks before the big surgery. She knew it was tentatively scheduled for the second week in November. With Jack away, she could schedule appointments before and after work, and therefore make doubly sure that she had all her bases covered. So, in addition to the spa, Rita, Karishma, Cree, and her chiropractor, she visited her primary care physician and her gynecologist, both of whom pronounced her the healthiest seriously ill person they had ever seen! Penney also increased her attendance at student activities and enjoyed a couple of concerts at the performing arts center. She worked with Jon and Sean, making certain they could assume any responsibility that might come their way during her upcoming absence.

Jack returned home, and together they went to Sirrah Glen for pre-op appointments with Dr. Saks, Dr. Tirion, and the anesthesiology team. The date for the surgery was set. They had only to wait.

VIII

E arly on a frosty November morning, a few days before her surgery, Penney stood in front of the bathroom mirror taking stock. She gazed at the person staring back at her, still not totally familiar with this image. Penney recognized only pieces of herself. She did have a nicely shaped head, when all was said and done. There were faint suggestions that her hair was trying once again to grow back. Her face was drawn and gaunt, however. Her skin was flaccidly pale. The old Penney from before cancer had always appeared full of life. This current Penney was hanging in there, but decidedly losing on some fronts.

And her chest…a study in the grotesque. Dr. Svensen admittedly had been right. Penney's once bouncy, beautiful breasts hung on her chest, the right one sadly hopeful, the left one misshapen and, well, ugly. Was it any wonder that Jack no longer desired her? Her abdomen, hips, and legs were more muscular than ever, though, and something to be proud of. Her toes did make her smile as she flashed back to a recent conversation with the anesthesiologist.

"I know you actually only need one nail bare for monitoring during surgery. I'll concede stripping my fingernails of color, but please let me wake up to a little color on my toes. It's really not too much to ask for either one of us." Penney peered expectantly at the attractive young woman facing her.

The anesthesiologist shook her head from side to side, her raven-black curls bouncing as she did so. A hint of a smile slowly formed on her face as she thoughtfully considered. "You know, you are right. You are absolutely right! Get yourself a really nice pedicure before the surgery. In fact, if you want to have clear polish on your fingernails, that's okay too."

One minor victory for Penney which she could chalk up. As Penney continued her reflections, she remembered the thrill of this success had made her boldly pose another of her wishes to Jack soon after the visit with the anesthesiologist. Sitting with Jack one evening watching television, Penney proffered her request to Jack during a commercial.

"Jack, I have been thinking that I would like Michael and Ginger here for my surgery."

Jack turned to look at her, a bit taken aback. "Why? I really don't think I need them here. They'll be extra work for me. You are going to need all of my attention."

"They wouldn't be here for an extended period of time. I would just like my children to be here. I'm frightened, Jack, and I thought having them here might be helpful for me and for you." Penney was fighting tears, blinking rapidly and swallowing hard.

Jack reached for her hand and patted it. "We'll be fine, Penney." He turned back to the television.

Penney's heart thudded all the way to the floor. In her mind, she heard that recurring slamming door banging again, and again, and again.

Penney could feel tears mounting once more as she went back over that conversation in her head. She would go into surgery with only her "roommate" by her side. Well, he was a damn good one most of the time, she had to admit. She quivered and moved away from the mirror. Her thoughts continued to revolve around shattered hopes and expectations as she prepared for the day. There would be no Ginger, no Michael by her side. Her parents had made minimal contact with her over the last couple of years, and it was now scarcer than ever. Jack would call them after the surgery, but both she and

Jack knew there would be little reaction. As Penney surveyed her final appearance, she took a deep breath. Yes, she could see she was still pretty and strong, but the doubts and demons she could not seem to banish from her brain. Penney knew most viewed her as a tower of strength and resilience, but in her heart of hearts, she knew she was crumbling. *Smile, Penney! Damn it, smile! Get energy from your smile!* She smiled and went off to work.

Once at work that day, Penney knew she had to be especially grateful for Jon and Sean. The three of them enjoyed one another and worked synchronously every day, as did all of her office staff. Her teaching staff now kept a careful eye on her, albeit from afar. Amity remained a concerned and all-weather friend. Her alternative care providers were working their hearts out for her. All things considered, in the final analysis, her daily life was pretty good.

Frank came to see her on her final day at work to wish her well and to reassure her that all would be fine at the high school while she was away. He also reinforced that she was not to think about coming back to work until she knew she was really ready to return. Frank thought the world of this woman, and he was deeply concerned for her health.

Jon and Sean had arranged for the office staff to have a luncheon for her. While the chatter over lunch was lighthearted, the concern in everyone's faces was unmistakable. Several gave her extra-tight hugs before Penney left that day. The rest of the building, it seemed, however, was unaware she was leaving for an extended period of time that day.

Penney and Jack left early that afternoon for Sirrah Glen, Jack picking her up at the high school. Penney surprised herself and slept most of the way. There was no turning back. She knew all the procedures had been carefully planned.

Upon arriving in Sirrah Glen, they drove straight to Dr. Saks' office. There they met with Dr. Saks and several members of his team. Using ultrasound as a guide, Dr. Saks went over again what he would be doing, and then marked his part of the surgical site in pink. It was fairly extensive once she saw it outlined in color on her body. In fact, it was a bit frightening. Dr. Tirion would be adding his markings tomorrow morning.

Penney was overcome with an overwhelming tiredness. She actually fell asleep on the ride from the medical center to the hotel. Once at the hotel, though, Penney perked up. She was going to enjoy her dinner out with Jack. They agreed not to talk about tomorrow. There wasn't much more to say at this point, anyway. They enjoyed the food, the wine, and one another.

As Penney prepared for bed, she took one short, last look in the mirror. Down her cheek trickled a lone tear, which she quickly wiped away. *C'mon, Penney. You understand the procedures and why they need to be done. You've researched the whole thing. Your life is moving on.* Penney drew away from the mirror, took her prescribed medication, dressed quickly for bed, and fell into a dreamless sleep after Jack kissed her good night.

Jack had Penney at the hospital bright and early the next morning, in fact, before dawn. The surgery itself was to begin at six AM and was expected to take at least eight hours. Penney was nervous but managed to hold her own in the pre- surgery banter with the various team members who would be assisting with her procedures. Since it was a teaching hospital, this was quite a crew, with surgeons, doctors, nurses, anesthesiologists, fellows, residents, students, and many others. The prep area around her was buzzing.

When Dr. Tirion arrived to mark his areas, Penney did find herself a little rattled. He added to Dr. Saks' markings on her left front chest wall in a different color, and then he moved to her back, where the *latissimus dorsi* was to be used to make the flap in preparation for her reconstructed breast. His pen seemed to fill her back as he drew a long line ending with a final flourish. Penney sucked her breath in, truly startled. She visualized the drawings she had studied for this part of the procedure, but still found herself silently asking just how extensive this mutilation was actually going to be. Studying the procedure was one thing, but this marking of her body made it all scathingly real. Her medications were starting to kick in, and she could feel her body growing heavy. She felt Jack's lips touch hers, and then nothing.

Penney could hear her name being called from a distance, but she was so tired, and her eyes just would not open. She could sense that there seemed to be a lot of activity going on around her: people moving into her space and out of it, much muffled conversation. There was also an overriding wail that permeated the air around her. A skirmish and a scuffle ensued, and she was certain she heard Jack's voice. *Ah, Jack...*

"You can arrest me if you want, but first I am going to find my wife." Jack's voice was angry, urgent.

"Sir, you can't be in here. Please come with us."

Dr. Saks' head jerked up from Penney's bedside. "Huh, wait! Let that man in here. Mr. Divan, I am so sorry..." Dr. Saks motioned for Jack to come forward and waved off the security personnel.

"At eight o'clock this evening, you told me I should be seeing Penney soon. It's now almost midnight. I have been searching for her since ten o'clock, when everyone else left the waiting area." As Jack moved toward Penney, he gasped as her face came into view.

Penney's face was ashen, her eyes encased in dark, hollowed circles, her lips tinged blue. Her breathing was shallow, and Jack could barely discern her chest moving beneath all the bandages and equipment covering and encircling her.

"What the fuck?" Jack spat his anger at all those around Penney's bed. The eerie wail in the background was increasing in intensity.

"Mr. Divan, as I told you earlier this evening, Penney is doing well. The surgery was more extensive than I believe any of us anticipated it would be. These first hours are critical, as are the next couple of days. We want Penney to be comfortable, and we are all carefully watching her. I can assure you she is receiving and will receive the best of care." Dr. Saks' exhaustion was evident in his voice.

Penney's eyes flickered as she found her voice and managed to whisper, "Jack?"

Jack was by her side, taking her hand, and planting a gentle kiss on her cold lips. All stepped back as Penney and Jack held each other's gaze for a few seconds in a tender, loving virtual caress. Penney tried to smile, but that effort alone caused her eyes to flutter and then close as she drifted back to sleep.

Jack turned to ask the group, "Why does she look like this? And what is that incessant noise?"

A couple of the members of the anesthesiology team explained that with the length of the surgery and with the nature of the medications used, blood flow in particular would manifest this way. However, at no time was she in any danger, and it would all clear up in a short amount of time. Dr. Saks added that it was probably best to prepare Penney to move upstairs as soon as possible, as another patient in the recovery area seemed to be in some distress. Under Dr. Saks and Dr. Tirion's supervision, the medical team had Penney ensconced in a room in a quiet corner of the intensive care unit in twenty minutes. Each remaining member of the team then proceeded to check wounds, sutures, drains, and IVs. Dr. Tirion used a flashlight to carefully survey the flap. As each finished his or her piece of the inspection, they left the room.

With the last member gone, Jack was left alone with Penney, who now slept soundly. She looked so small and so frail amidst all the paraphernalia surrounding her. Monitors cast a ghoulish glow over Penney's head while they ticked off data and kept track of numerous bodily functions and fluids. Jack sat and put his head on Penney's abdomen and was soon breathing evenly with her. He woke a couple of hours later when he heard the nurse requesting, "Sir, I must check her vitals, her flap, her drains…"

"Sure. Sure. I'll just step out." In the hallway, Jack stretched his arms over his head and walked a little. His mind was numb. The nurse beckoned from the doorway, indicating he could come back.

Jack took another look at Penney. He did believe he could see some color—well, a little color, anyway—seeping back into her face. He bent over, gave Penney a kiss, and softly tiptoed out of the room. He waved to the nurse, saying, "I'll be back later this morning." When he reached the hotel room, he fell onto the bed and immediately fell into a deep slumber.

Penney awakened to a pain so intense it took her breath away. She wasn't sure she could even move to find the nurse call button. She was packed snugly into the bed with pillows all around her. Her legs were swathed in inflatable leggings kneading away so that blood clots would not form. She had IV lines in both her right arm and her right foot. There were drains and pumps encircling her. From her bed, she called, "Help, please. Help." The wail, which she had thought was part of a nightmare last night, she could clearly make out, and it was not far away. She raised her voice: "Hellllp!"

A nurse soon appeared, asking, "Are you in pain? It is time for your pain meds." The nurse was young and blond, and seemed a little frantic.

"Yes, I am. What are you giving me?"

"Vicodin. Your chart says you will refuse morphine."

"Vicodin it is, then. No morphine. No, thank you."

When the nurse returned with Penney's meds, Penney asked if she could please have access to the call button. With a little rearranging, the nurse was able to locate it easily within Penney's reach. All this while, the wailing increased, and the nurse grew visibly more tense.

"If you are okay, I need to check on my other patient."

"I hope that person is going to be all right. All this has worn me out, so I'm going to rest some more." Penney smiled weakly at the nurse and was quickly back to sleep before the nurse even left the room.

Penney's drug-induced slumber was soon interrupted by doctors, surgeons, residents, and third-year medical students all making their rounds. She was repeatedly told to remain as still as possible while they peered at the flap with a flashlight, checked out the fluid output from her various drains, and discussed what to do next. Dr. Tirion's reconstruction team did ask if she had any questions, to which she readily responded.

"The pain is blitzing at the end of four hours."

"Well, morphine might help, but we know you are opposed to that."

"How about OxyContin?" inquired one of the residents.

"If she won't take morphine, I am guessing OxyContin is out of the question. Mrs. Divan?"

"You're right. No narcotics there can't be an alternative to, if it can be helped." Penney's energy was noticeably flagging at this point.

Dr. Tirion rubbed his chin and offered, "We are going to try an acetaminophen regimen, Penney. It may seem excessive at first, but this is for post-surgical pain that we need to move you beyond. I'll get the nurse started on this. You sleep now."

With that, the team filed out of the room. The nurse was back in the room in no time adding meds to Penney's IV. Penney fell back asleep almost immediately, lulled by a dream where her Reiki master, Cree, channeled the pain away from her body.

Penney reawakened to a screeching wail. *What on earth could be wrong with that patient?* She should probably be glad her pain did not lead to screaming. *And what is this? It looks like food…* Penney reached for the call button. No one came, and the noise got louder. Penney sighed and floated back into her dreams.

Next, Penney was gently roused by a nursing student who wanted to check her vitals. The young student looked warily at Penney's IV, as the vein was puffy and the skin around it an angry red. "I'm not sure that is going to make it through the day," she said as she pointed at the IV line. "Lucky you have another one ready to go." She then frowned at the gelatinous masses that were probably once breakfast. "Not hungry yet?" she inquired.

"I'm supposed to lie very still. Sitting up has not been offered as an option. I actually sorta want to get up. Is that possible?"

"Let me check." The student nurse bounced out of the room with a determined look.

She returned with the new day nurse assigned to Penney, who took one look at the situation and announced, "Okay! Let's see if we can't prop you up a little." That done, the RN asked if Penney wouldn't like to try a little water. Penney was brought a bathroom-size cup of water that wet her lips and quenched her dry throat.

"I'm going to order you something light to eat. I'll check with your doctors and see if we can't get you off this catheter. I apologize, but we are going to have to move your IV line to that other site. Now let's get you a little more presentable. I was told by the night nurse that your husband would return later this morning."

The two nurses deftly changed the sheets and Penney's gown. She was served a bowl of Cream of Wheat, which she dabbled at. There were more vitals and drains, and the flap was checked again. The IV line now extended from her foot. The vein chosen was right next to a bone, now adding a new discomfort. Penney was growing tired again, and soon her eyes were closed, her breathing soft but regular.

When Jack arrived, he found Penney resting peacefully. A faint tinge of pink could be made out on her cheeks, though the grayish-blue cast still remained, particularly around her eyes. Jack sat in the chair beside the bed and perused the bed scene. *Good God! What have they done to her? At least the blood-ridden gown has vanished.* He slipped out to get her some flowers. He was pretty sure he had caught a glimpse of a bouquet of daisies in his peripheral vision when he passed the gift shop.

That little shopping trip took him twenty minutes, and then he was back in Penney's room. He bent over the bed to kiss her, causing her eyes to pop open.

"Jack." Penney smiled.

"Penney, I do love you!" He held out the bouquet made up of white daisies and baby's breath.

Penney's smile grew. "My favorite, daisies!"

The nurse entered the room at this point. "I'll just take those. I think we will set them right over here, so Mrs. Divan can see them. How's the pain, Mrs. Divan?"

"Growing. And this IV is really irritating." Penney looked at the snatched bouquet wistfully.

The nurse adjusted the IV a little, saying there wasn't much wiggle room, and then she went off to get Penney's meds.

"Jack, when you get a chance, could you please get me a latte? I've had water and Cream of Wheat, and now I'm ready for my old standby. Could you also put those flowers nearer to me so I can enjoy them up close?" Penney spoke softly as Jack held her hand.

Returning with the meds, the nurse wanted to know if Penney wanted to sit up on the edge of the bed for just a bit. After removing Penney's inflatable leggings, the nurse slowly brought Penney to a sitting position, instructing her to sit still for a moment. Penney did so, and then, carefully and very deliberately, the nurse guided Penney to move her hips and then her legs over the side of the bed. Jack held onto her hand the whole time.

"How are you doing, Mrs. Divan?"

"Please call me Penney. I'm feeling a little wobbly and woozy."

"Okay. Just a few more moments."

Penney took three breaths and then shook her head at the nurse. The nurse eased Penney back into bed; replaced the inflatable leggings; checked vitals, drains, IV, and flap; and made Penney as comfortable as she could. Jack stood nearby feeling rather helpless. He held his breath a couple of times.

"Good job, Penney! A little later, we'll remove that catheter. By this afternoon, we'll have you take your husband for a walk. Now, get some rest." As she spoke, the nurse gave Jack a look he understood.

Penney and Jack watched her leave the room and then looked at one another. They heaved a collective sigh.

"Okay, Penney, you take a little nap. I'm going to catch up on some e-mails, make some phone calls, and go in search of your latte. Let me just move that bouquet a little closer for you." He placed Penney's flowers on her nightstand.

"Fabulous!" Penney was fighting sleep as they spoke.

Jack waved on his way out. Penney was able to feebly blow him a kiss. As Penney slid back into sleep, she realized the wailing had stopped. There remained a blissful quiet. Yet, what had happened to that patient?

As the day wore on, the catheter was removed. Penney was able to get out of bed, though preparing her took longer than the actual jaunts to the restroom or the chair in her room. The first few trips left her worn out, but by early evening, she could actually sit up for a while afterward and read or converse. She could only glean from the nurse that the other patient had been moved to an acute care unit.

The medical team remained vigilant with their monitoring. Jack brought not one, but two lattes through the course of the day, as Penney took one look at the bland lunch served to her and said, "No, thank you." Future meals would fare little better. Wishes for a healthy recovery came in by e-mail and cell phone. Jack kept his visits short, as Penney tired so easily. That night, Penney slept well—that is, when they were not waking her to check on the status of everything.

The next morning, Penney remained awake after rounds and the nursing shift change. She was feeling a little desperate to get cleaned up. Pushing the call button, she smiled a little. She was beginning to take charge of herself again.

Another, different young nurse appeared. This one was tall, thin, and wore her hair in a very long, cascading ponytail. "How may I help you this morning?" the nurse offered as she eyed Penney's uneaten breakfast.

"I would really like to get cleaned up a little. Is that possible?" Penney looked at the nurse entreatingly.

"Well, absolutely! Let's start by getting you unhooked from a few things."

That ordeal done, the nurse helped Penney out of bed and into the bathroom. A stool awaited Penney, along with soap, towels, toothbrush, toothpaste, and comb. *Really? A comb?* Penney asked for her bag and laid out a few more things as the nurse announced on her way out that Penney could use the call button when she was done.

Penney looked at the back of the retreating nurse, wondering, *What? No assistance? No monitoring? I can barely get in and out of bed without help. Now I'm left sitting on a three-legged stool by myself. Well, okay, then!* Penney carefully pulled the gown down off her shoulders. She had been instructed not to pull anything over her head. Grasping the counter in front of her, Penney took a good, long look. Bandages covered most of her chest and her back. Where bandages did not appear, tape held drains in place, as well as a pain pump. She had her suspicions that the pain pump contained morphine. In the area where they checked the flap, there was a nubbin of skin left protruding. *Totally unattractive! And what about my face? I look like a faded Smurf!* Penney sighed, wet her washcloth, and carefully washed what she could of her body, starting with her downy scalp. Afterward, she applied eye cream, moisturizer, and body lotion where possible. She had to admit she felt much better. Putting on a fresh gown, Penney took a last look in the mirror, shook her head, and then closed her eyes. The gift of life would be her one beautiful thing for the day. As she and the IV pole shuffled back into the bedroom, the nurse came rambling in with meds and pillows.

"Wow! You look like a whole new person! Is that lavender I smell? It's nice! Let's check you out now once we get you back in bed and reattached." The nurse hummed as she began the process. She indicated all looked well when she gave Penney's pillows each a final pat before settling them strategically around Penney.

Jack entered the room as the nurse left. He looked Penney up and down and declared, "Penney, you are coming back to the land of the living." Giving her a kiss, he added, "You smell good, too! That's my girl!" He gave her another kiss and squeezed her hand.

"Jack, why am I blue? And my eyes…"

"Trust me, Penney, you look a thousand percent better than you did yesterday."

"But…"

"No buts, Penney. You really do look better."

The two of them chatted about inconsequential things then, until lunch arrived. Jack took one look at the lumps of white and said, "Penney, I'm on this. Give me about thirty minutes. I'll be back."

During the intervening time, Penney took a peek at the nubbin again. *Well, the* pectoralis major *and* minor *are gone, but good grief! What a whole lot of me is missing!* Penney shuddered and leaned deep into the pillow behind her, breathing rhythmically and clearing her mind.

"Mrs. Divan, hello."

Penney opened her eyes to a trio of residents she recognized from the reconstruction team. She had dubbed them Winkin', Blinkin', and Nod based upon their behaviors during rounds. One was short and sported a buzz cut. Another was tall, dark, but not handsome, too chiseled and angular. The third was of average build, could be cocky when interacting with the team, and offered information pretty readily when the team was quizzed.

"Hello, gentlemen," she said tiredly.

"Mind if we take a look at you?" Nod asked.

"I'm all yours," Penney sighed.

Once they had finished their exam, Penney took a deep breath and asked, "Do you know what Dr. Tirion plans to do with this?" as she pointed at the small, projecting piece of skin.

They shuffled their feet and looked at one another, each, in turn, winking, blinking, and nodding. They collectively shrugged their shoulders and in unison replied, "No...but we will ask."

"I would appreciate that," said Penney as she showered them with her smile.

"Well, see you around," said Winkin'. They each waved as they left the room.

Penney returned briefly to her silent meditation. She heard Jack's footsteps even before he entered the room.

"Penney, I found your favorite coffee shop and got us both one of those veggie sandwiches you like," Jack bubbled as he excitedly unwrapped the fresh vegetables carefully encased between two slices of freshly baked whole-grain bread. "Voila!"

Penney sat up, realizing that she was actually hungry. She picked up her sandwich, brought it to her lips, and savored that first bite. Pure bliss was written on her face as she announced, "Brilliant! Jack, you are brilliant! Is that a latte in the other bag?"

"Yes, ma'am! Let's enjoy!"

They continued their earlier conversation until the nurse came in. "I really didn't think our hospital food was that bad, but I do have to say that what you have there looks delicious. You're eating, too! I'll be back to check everything after your lunch."

Penney and Jack finished their sandwiches and coffee. The nurse returned to check Penney's vitals, her drains, and her flap, and finally to dispense medications. Jack helped the nurse make Penney comfortable and then took his leave for the afternoon while Penney slept.

The afternoon and evening brought a familiar sameness with careful monitoring and a steady improvement in Penney's appearance and in her energy levels. Jack returned with a hearty vegetable soup for Penney's dinner and a chocolate croissant for her breakfast. They laughed a little over dinner at Chez Penney's Room. Before Jack left for the night, Penney had him promise to bring her computer in with him the next morning.

Penney woke early to the sounds of the reconstruction team gathering outside her room. Dr. Tirion entered first.

"Good morning, Penney! You are looking lovely this morning. I hear you have questions for me." He smiled while the others lined up alongside her bed.

"Yes, thank you. I was wondering what your plans are for this little piece here." Penney slid her gown slightly off her shoulder to expose the dangling piece of skin.

"Well, Penney, you know yours was not our typical mastectomy. We need to have your flap continue to heal as well as it has been. Your pain pump is empty, so I'll remove that this morning. I'm going to keep you here in the ICU a couple more days so we can keep a very close eye on you, have you build up a little more strength, and ask that you eat a little more. This time next week, I will see you in my office to take a look at you and start planning for injections to your expander to gradually fill it. This little nubbin we'll have to address further down the line. In the meantime, you and I have a lot to do. Okay?" His smile was not wavering.

"Yes, I guess. It's just a lot to take in." Penney could feel a pout coming on. Dr. Tirion had explained his plan, and that was that. She could also see that his team was taking their lead from Winkin',

Blinkin', and Nod and politely engaging in like- minded nonverbal activities.

"All right. Let's get that pump out and take a look at you."

Penney did not even feel the pump's line coming out. In fact, she didn't feel much of anything. She tried clearing her mind and focusing on her breathing, but the exam covered her chest and her back and required her physical participation. Penney was glad to see this team file out so that she could prepare for the day. She needed to wash the clinical touch of others away. She was especially pleased to see Jack arrive later that morning with her computer in tow.

After lunch, Penney sent e-mails to Frank, Jon and Sean, her secretaries, Ginger and Ken, Michael, Amity, and Hannah. She got pretty immediate responses from each of them, all bringing a smile to her face. Next, she called the nurse and asked to go for a walk around the unit. It was slow, but she knew she would pick up speed on her next circuit, which she did with Jack later in the day. Penney realized as she prepared for bed that evening that she wanted to go home.

Arising on day four, Penney vowed she would get herself out of here as quickly as possible. She called the night nurse to unleash her so that she could get herself ready for the day prior to rounds. Sitting in the chair beside her bed while sipping prune juice, Penney was found lost in thought by Dr. Saks.

"Hello, Penney. You look great! How are you feeling?"

Penney looked up to say, "Hey! Where have you been? I know your team has been in to see me, but I have missed you."

"Ah, Penney, you have been in good hands. Dr. Tirion and I have talked every day. Dr. Salvatore has called to check on you every day as well. Just look at you!"

Dr. Saks examined Penney and repeatedly told Penney how well she was doing.

Penney had to ask then, "Do you think I can go home?"

"That is for Dr. Tirion to determine. You have had quite an experience, so if I were you, I would take advantage of this level of care."

"Oh, I know. I just want my own things to wear, my own comfy furniture to lounge in. I want my music to listen to.

"Well, why don't we have Jack bring you in a pair of pajamas? I'll call him myself if you like. I'd like to tell him how well you are looking."

"Sure, give him a call."

Penney looked at Dr. Saks quizzically. *He seemed to be saying that his was not the primary role in this whole procedure. Odd...* "So, Dr. Saks, will I be seeing you again soon?"

"Actually, Penney, I will see you in my office next week. My office will try to coordinate with Dr. Tirion's office so that you can see us both on the same day."

"Well, from my perspective, it does sound like my release is coming up."

"Yes, indeed. Now, I'm going to go give Jack a call. I'll see if I can't get him to bring you some pajamas. Rest and be well." Dr. Saks disappeared through the doorway.

Penney snuggled into her pillows. Finding any comfortable position was still proving elusive. For one split second, though, she could feel the pillows wrap around her like angels' wings, soothing and caressing. Penney shut her eyes and let sleep take over.

When she woke, the pain was growing, but she actually felt rested. Penney called the nurse for meds, made herself presentable, and walked several circuits around the unit. As she neared her room on the last lap, Jack appeared with a package in hand.

"Sorry I'm a little late. Dr. Saks seemed to think I needed to do a little shopping. Jack grinned as he handed over the shopping bag.

Penney quickly grinned herself as she pulled out a pair of leopard-printed flannel pajamas with hot-pink piping.

"These will certainly liven up this place. What do you think?" she asked as she held the pajama top up in front of her chest.

"I saw them, and they were just screaming your name. Dr. Saks thought you needed a little cheering up. Here you have it!"

"I'll have them on for dinner."

Penney and Jack chatted about everything under the sun until Penney began to tire. Jack gave her a kiss and left her to rest. As he walked down the hall, he found himself thinking. Her color was steadily returning, though her eyes were still faintly bruised-looking. He also sensed she was brooding about something. In the final analysis, all he knew was that she was alive and recovering. Jack whistled on his way down in the elevator.

Penney had the nurse help her change for dinner. The pajama top had to be worn backward so that the drains could be monitored and emptied, the flap area easily accessed, and the *latissimus dorsi* scar checked. The pajama bottoms felt good wrapped around her legs. When her transformation was complete, Penney did feel uplifted. Now, if she could just go home…

On cue, Dr. Tirion's team showed up. She assisted them with her checkup. When they asked if she had any questions, she looked around at all of them pleadingly. "This IV in my foot is a constant source of irritation. Surely what medication I am being given now, I could be given orally."

"It's hospital policy to administer medication in the ICU intravenously." They all nodded their heads in agreement. "But we'll check," one added while another interjected, "Mrs. Divan, you are looking lovely this evening."

"Thank you, gentlemen," Penney replied as they quietly took their leave.

Only twenty minutes later, the nurse came in to say that they would be removing the IV in the morning, and very likely moving her to a larger unit, provided all her vitals and incisions were good. Penney was elated and went right out to do more laps around the unit.

When Jack returned, he found Penney looking, as he said, "pretty as a picture." Learning of her impending release from the IV, he could sense that brooding lifting from her a little. He discovered a new sense of relief himself. He would be taking her home very soon.

The new dawn did bring a move for Penney and the removal of her IV. Dr. Tirion said she might be able to go home the next day.

Jon and Sean called her on Skype, and the three of them discussed a couple of employee issues that were surfacing. Penney was returning to business.

Later in the day, a new nurse appeared to introduce herself. She was of average height, wore her light-brown hair at shoulder length, and spoke with a heavy southern accent. She also carried a package of tubing, needles, and—*Yikes!*—a cannula.

"What is this for? asked Penney, her eyes narrowing, her shoulders held defensively, and pointing at the IV set.

"Well, it will soon be time for your meds, and they are to be administered by IV," the nurse responded matter-of-factly, busying herself with arranging the package on the counter, not sensing a storm arising.

Penney immediately broke in, shouting, "They are not! Not! Not! The IV was removed this morning, and I am to take all medications orally. If you come near me with that, you are going to be in danger of committing a felony. Now out! Out! Out!" Penney's face was a purplish color, her heart thumped, and her voice continued to rise with every word she spoke.

The nurse backed out of the room, speechless, though her mouth was wide open.

Penney sobbed from the depths of her being and noisily for quite some time. She felt like she had been stripped and beaten. When Jack arrived, he hugged her and let her cry herself out. Then, through hiccups, she explained what had happened. He tucked her into bed and went to find the nurse. She too was in tears, and Jack made her cry more as he insisted upon an apology from her to Penney.

After several nurses at the nurses' station studied Penney's chart, they all had to admit that it did indeed indicate that Penney had doctor's orders to take all her meds orally. The nurse in question wiped her tears, blew her nose, and stood up. Looking directly at Jack, she pleaded for forgiveness.

Jack returned her direct look and evenly stated, "I am not the one you have to offer an apology to."

The nurse cast her eyes down and softly said, "I am so very sorry." She shuffled off in the direction of Penney's room.

Penney searched the doorway with her eyes when she heard footsteps tentatively approaching her door. The nurse appeared in the doorway, puffy red eyes masking her features. Penney glowered at her.

The nurse spoke in a low voice to explain, "I am very sorry for upsetting you. All of my other patients are always administered their meds with an IV."

Penney stared at the nurse aghast as she said, "It is always dangerous to make assumptions."

"Yes. Yes. You are right. I am so very, very sorry." With that said, the nurse left the room, never to be seen again. Another nurse quickly and cheerily came into Penney's room with pills and water. Jack followed shortly thereafter, and he held Penney for a long time. They both pulled away when they realized the room had grown dark, as had the sky outside.

IX

P enney was able to leave the hospital by nine the next morning. She left with bruises, bandages, drains, and a tissue expander, as well as a stern admonition from Dr. Tirion to take it easy. He knew all about her workouts and her passion for her job. He also knew keeping his fingers crossed wasn't going to do the trick. *She is one tough lady,* he thought as he watched her husband help her into the front seat of a shiny, black Mercedes.

Penney felt the cool morning air on her face and closed her eyes to feel and to hear the air swirl around her. The crispness of the morning and the bustle about her filled her senses as she eased into the front seat.

"Ready?" Jack asked, looking himself to double-check that Penney was secure.

"Oh, yes! Let's please go!" Penney directed giddily.

Penney fell asleep in the car. Before she knew it, Jack was announcing, "We're home!"

He helped her out of the car, but Penney rushed to open the back door to their home—*her own busy house reflecting her busy life.*

"It is good to be home," she said as she collapsed into an oversized armchair in the living room. "I shall sit and enjoy this chair for a while." Penney smiled, deep in thought, as she looked at the art hanging on the walls, all meaningful to her as they were bought at times both she and Jack wanted to remember. She paused over *"Loving Embrace,"* a portrait of two Native Americans whose eyes and arms locked them in a tender moment. *Ah, well...* thought Penney as she twisted her head to study the painting. *Those moments so captured the endurance of love and time itself. True love went far deeper than the physical.*

Penney looked away as Jack called from the kitchen, "How about a salad for lunch?"

"Sure," said Penney, now delighting in just stretching her toes.

"Can I get you anything before I get started making the salads?" Jack still talked from the next room.

"A throw and my computer would be good."

"You got it!" Jack quickly brought her a snowy white throw which he smoothed over her legs, and her computer which he held back a moment. "Remember what Dr. Tirion said. You are to take it slow, so you have an hour for now. Okay?"

"Uh-huh," Penney replied as she reached for the laptop.

Jack shook his head as he walked out of the room.

Penney called Frank on Skype, and he answered immediately.

"Well, well, well, Mrs. Divan! I see you are looking pretty perky this afternoon. Jon and Sean have informed me that they have already consulted you on a personnel issue. I have taken the liberty to approve half days for you to work, but I want you working from home. And that does mean four hours a day, tops."

"Thank you! Thank you, Frank! You're a peach! Any other projects you want me looking at?" Penney's face was lighting up, and Frank could see the color rising on her face.

"Yes. Please follow my instructions – four hours, no more, from home. Now get some rest."

Frank signed off, and Jack appeared to announce that lunch was ready. He reiterated Frank's instructions over lunch, adding that he thought two hours in the morning and two in the afternoon really should be the plan.

"Okay. I've got it! In fact, I'm going to rest right now." Jack followed along to the bedroom to empty drains and to see that Penney was comfortable.

Jack himself was happy to return to work in his office at home. He caught up on emails and made phone calls. A couple of hours into his work, he heard Penney moving about downstairs.

"You okay down there?" he called out.

"I'm fine, Jack. I'll be in the living room."

Penney opened her laptop, looked over her emails, and sent an e-mail to Jon and Sean. They responded quickly. Penney called them on Skype.

"Hey, guys!"

"Wow! Hey! Frank said you wouldn't waste any time getting back to work," Sean offered as he carefully looked Penney over. Still the mistress of disguises, he could garner. She was visibly tired, but animated and looking her stylish self in jeans, blouse, and coordinated scarf.

Jon went right to the topic at hand. "We need to pick your brain for a bit regarding the forever-ongoing feud between the guidance department and the math department. You said guidance might abuse the variety of math options you created, and we think that is happening."

"Give me a few specifics," Penney said as she readied paper and pen to take notes.

"A couple of the guidance counselors of late seem to be trying selected students out in your less-accelerated math classes because, in their words, the students' parents want their kids to be successful."

"Are these students capable of being successful in their original math classes?"

"Oh yes!" Jon and Sean answered in unison.

"The numbers are to be kept very low in these new classes. Are they trying to exceed the maximum?"

"Yes again, but so far we have not allowed it. A few of the parents, though, are clamoring pretty loudly."

"Okay. Let me send an e-mail to the guidance department chair. I'll copy you both so she can see we are talking."

"Thanks, Penney!"

Yes! And thank you guys!"

The three of them moved on to other topics for a while, ending with both men telling Penney they missed her but hoped she would take it slow.

Penney got right to her e-mail, beginning with a generic greeting and then moving right into the issue:

> From: Penney Divan
> To: Janise Porter
>
> I would love to meet with you in person, but I am homebound for a while. It has come to my attention that the new math classes are full, and there is a waiting list. I want to reiterate that these new classes were created for those students who have demonstrated that they do not have the basic math skills necessary to be successful in higher-order math classes. These new classes are designed to prepare particular students to be successful in our more rigorous math classes. They do not replace our core math curriculum, nor are they appropriate for those students who chose not to do the work in the higher-order math classes. Please remember my mantra when dealing with students and their parents who are interested in getting an easy grade: having to work hard is not a detriment to college-bound or career-bound students.
>
> Should you have any questions, please e-mail or call me.
>
> Have a good day!
>
> Penney

This was sent after proofreading and copied to Jon and Sean. Penney knew guidance counselors walked a fine line sometimes, trying to appease students and their parents and working side-by-side with their colleagues on the staff. In the end, the guidance counselors, for the most part, were good, well-meaning people who unintentionally sometimes drew rancor for what appeared to be alienating behaviors when they were really trying to help.

Hmmph! thought Penney. She leaned back in her chair, overcome with the recurring realization that far too many people had no idea how lives could be turned upside down when decisions did not meet expectations or consequences did not jibe with events. The insularity of others was often disconcerting. Leaning back relaxed her body, however, and she soon fell into a peaceful repose.

Jack shook her gently to wake her.

Smiling at Jack, Penney said, "Jack, you have no idea how I have been missing this room. Let's open the front door for just a minute, so I can hear the pond."

For a brief moment, each knew the true meaning of serenity. They leaned into one another and drank in the sounds of silence. The silence brought with it the flow of the water, the rustling of the breeze, and the beat of their hearts. This led the way to a restful evening, a reward they both agreed they had earned.

As Penney began her preparations for the new day the next morning, she looked at the flap area in horror. It was black where the day before it had presented a bruised appearance. She walked directly to the phone and speed-dialed the hospital, asking for the cosmetic/reconstruction surgery resident on duty. A familiar voice greeted her, though who it was by name she could not say. Penney explained what she was seeing and then waited for a reply. She knew he must be pulling up her file on the computer.

"Hi, Mrs. Divan. I was there for your final exit exam, and everything looked fine. It would be very unlikely to change so quickly. I'm sending a text to Dr. Tirion right now. I do suspect he will want to see you. Will you be able to have someone drive you back down?"

"Yes, of course." Penney was not liking any of this.

"Great! Give me your number so Dr. Tirion can text you directly. I'm sure it's fine, but it's better to be on the safe side. Bye now."

When Penney turned around, Jack was standing behind her. "Sounds like we may be going for a ride."

"Sorry."

"No, I don't like the looks of that either. Let's get cleaned up so we are ready to go."

Go they did. Dr. Tirion pronounced the area well, just blood accumulation at the wound. He did assure Penney and Jack that he did have to physically see it and thanked them for making the trip. Penney and Jack then returned home. Their lives were getting used to incorporating these types of events as part of their regular routine, and more importantly, not letting these events interfere with their work and daily lives. Penney was on her laptop and phone to and from Sirrah Glen. Jack worked on his laptop while Penney saw Dr. Tirion. He fielded phone calls before and after lunch and made his usual number of contacts following dinner.

Penney looked for a response from the guidance department chair. Penney's response from Janise was brief, saying she understood. She did wonder if Penney could participate in a couple of pre-Thanksgiving break parent conferences. Penney agreed to do these via Skype.

The upcoming weekend brought a welcome respite. On Sunday, however, Doug and Kate showed up with a complete dinner and entertained Penney and Jack through the afternoon. It appeared Kate had not cut her hair, but Penney wasn't going to ask. Penney had to admit that she was a little spent after their visit. It was very unlike Doug and Kate to show up unannounced, but Penney and Jack agreed that they were glad they did. It was what many of their friends would have done previously, in the time before Penney's cancer. It was indeed "just what the doctor ordered!"

Penney put in her usual work hours Monday and Tuesday, including the promised parent-teacher conferences via Skype. These went very well, with the parents grateful for Penney's input and for her participation. The students remained in their classes, and they promised to perform to the best of their abilities.

Monday evening, her acupuncturist, Karishma, made a home visit, took one look at Penney after greeting her with a long hug, and said, "Sweet Spirit! What wonders this western medicine can manifest! Let's get to work!" Penney journeyed in her mind to the far reaches of the universe while the needles did their magic. That is, up to a point, for as often happened on this type of journey, Penney would reach the ends of the universe lit up by a scorching sunset behind doors just barely open, and then they would slam shut, one by one.

Penney had explored this imagery with her spiritual healer, but ultimately only Penney held the answer. She did not have the answer, but she was certain it lay beyond those doors. As the final door shut, Penney opened her eyes, and Karishma reentered the room.

"How'd you do?" asked Karishma.

"Fine, until I get to the door thing."

"Yours is all about the heart. Spend some time contemplating your fourth chakra. Remember, Penney, that central to Chinese medicine is the notion that the heart is the regulator of the entire human being. Your renewal regarding your sense of peace begins today, and it begins by revitalizing and making your heart stronger physically and spiritually. Now let's see what your pulses did."

Karishma held Penney's tiny wrist in her hand and smiled as she noted a significant change. "Great pulse change!" Karishma also went over how important it was for Penney to gradually ease into activities, reminding her it was okay to just *be*. She made an appointment in a couple of weeks to see Penney in her office. As Karishma pulled away from Penney's home, she said a blessing. This woman captivated her. She would see to it that Penney grew stronger. Now, how to make her free?

Tuesday evening, a couple of the technicians from the spa brought smiles and nail polish to do a manicure and pedicure, and, of course, to make Penney laugh. It hurt a little to laugh, but it sure did free up a lot of happy endorphins needing to be released.

Wednesday, Penney and Jack made the trip to Sirrah Glen. The roads were clear of snow and traffic. It was the day before Thanksgiving. Dr. Tirion removed her stitches and her three remaining drains. He reminded Penney that she should watch for fever, chills, odor at any of the surgical sites, a rash, and nausea. He explained that he had added a hundred cubic centimeters of saline to her tissue expander at the time of surgery. They would wait for a month or so before more was added. She was to let her scars heal on their own for now.

When Penney broached the topic of activities, Dr. Tirion folded his arms across his chest (never a good sign), stared directly at Penney, and rapidly stated, "You are not to exercise your upper body. You may walk or use the stationary bike within limits. If you are tired, rest. You can work half days, but if you are tired, go home. Don't lie on your chest. Be careful, Penney. Please don't push yourself. Your surgery was major, and your recovery and healing will necessarily be major too."

Penney stared right back at him. "I'm tight all over my chest and back. This swelling is a little frightening. I feel lumpy in odd places."

"This all takes time. We will do our part, and we need you to do yours. Be patient. And rest, please rest."

Jack had been listening carefully. "I'll do my best to hold her down."

Everyone laughed. They all shook hands and wished one another each a happy Thanksgiving. Penney and Jack went on to see Dr. Saks. He was happy to see the two of them. Penney looked well, he quickly noted. This visit was relatively short and mundane. They talked about future scans, mammograms, and when her care should return to Dr. Salvatore.

Penney and Jack were once again off to return home to prepare for their yearly visit to see Jack's mother. From hospital to home to medical center to home and then to the airport and Mountain View. From the outside, it might have appeared to be a lot, but no one seemed to be paying much attention. For Penney and Jack, it was now status quo. It all simply happened, had to happen.

Jack's mother had aged a little in the past year, and her emphysema and COPD were wreaking a greater toll on her body and stamina. In spite of it all, she still displayed a sharp mind and a ready wit. She did indeed maintain her part in the repartee at the family Thanksgiving dinner. Penney was quieter than usual but was ever ready to help with final preparations, serving, and cleanup. Jack took good care of the wine service at dinner and ribbed his cousins unmercifully. Later, during the long weekend, his cousins would join him at his mother's house and help with repairing the sprinkler system, the door locks, and a few other odds and ends around the house, all of which Penney supervised. As usual, absolutely no one would say or ask anything about Penney's health. It had to be some convoluted, unwritten taboo, Penney and Jack had decided. The weekend came to an end, and Penney and Jack were once again on the road.

Jack decided on the way home from the airport that he and Penney would stop and have dinner at one of their many favorite restaurants. As they settled in with a toast to the long weekend, Jack announced, "I have a little surprise for you, Penney. Tomorrow, Ginger and Ken will be arriving to spend some time with us. You need some help decorating for the holidays, I was thinking. Ginger also can be pretty persuasive when she wants to be..."

Penney interrupted, "Jack, thank you." She looked directly at him as her eyes filled with tears. "Just so you know, these are tears of happiness." She bowed her head, took a deep breath, and wiped her eyes, and then together she and Jack enjoyed bouillabaisse with a zinfandel made from old vine grapes. Penney's heart was happy.

Ginger and Ken arrived just ahead of a snowstorm. The new-fallen snow brought a peaceful restfulness to the landscape. That landscape beckoned to the four of them, and answering that invitation, the four of them created a snowman worthy of the Frosty lore. Once finished admiring their handiwork, they then placed themselves on the ground around the snowman to offer snow angels as his permanent visitors. It was a pure invitation to have some fun. Next, the holiday decorating began. There were dozens of miniature holiday characters to set around the house. Wreaths had to be chosen for the mailbox, the lamp post, and the front door. The fireplace mantel turned out to be an artful celebration strewn with fresh pine boughs, shimmery ornaments collected over many years, and tiny trees dressed in glitter. The whole house shone under Penney's orchestration. Each stood back to admire their collective decorative prowess and to raise their mugs of eggnog in a toast to beauty and life.

"To Penney, my brave mistress of enduring beauty," declared Jack, blowing a kiss Penney's way.

"To Penney, don't ever let this knock you down," added Ken with a nod of his head.

"To Mom, please stay well. I'd really like to travel with you again. And, well, we all need you," offered Ginger thoughtfully.

"To all three of you, for helping me with this. I couldn't have done this without you." Penney smiled at each of them and then led the way to the kitchen, where the lasagna pan bubbled in the oven and the garlic bread awaited preparation.

That night, Penney lay awake for a long time. Her chest and back hurt. Okay, maybe she had overdone a bit today, but she was so pleased to have Ginger here that it was hard to contain her happiness. Her smile faded as the thought struck her—*Yet, I am so sad...* Penney knew at this moment she had to let some things go in order to truly restore balance in her life. Her strength would have to be more internal than ever before. Losing the *pectoralis* muscles could potentially impact her physical strength. Parts of her workout would have to be rethought. She would need to further grow in practicing mindfulness in order to build a reservoir of internal strength. That strength she would need to bring to her workplace. Her staff would continue to watch her, she knew, and her resourcefulness would be assessed before they responded.

Ginger and Ken, Michael, and her parents all needed space to find their way with her illness too in their own time. Jack loved her, she was certain, but all this impacted his work, and he could be resentful at times. What would he think of her body now that it had undergone a complete pentimento, the final alteration not yet complete? What further permutations awaited her? She had often gone much of this alone. Penney knew she had to be strong for herself first.

So many were confounded by her disease. It would be up to her to make it less perplexing, quite honestly not just for others but for herself as well. Should she try to live a life as seemingly disease-free?

That would be a lie. After all, she had eschewed wearing her wig this time around! Penney had been on a roller coaster ride of teetering determination for a couple of years now. This she now knew: her resolve had to become steadfast. She would work toward achieving a decisiveness that revolved around being strong in body, mind, and spirit. Penney had to show herself and others what triumphant looked like. A heady resolution it was, but absolutely necessary. Penney closed her eyes, took three long, lingering breaths, and slept soundly through the remainder of the night. The next morning, the sun made the snow glisten, and her heart opened to the start of a new day.

X

Tuesday, Ginger and Ken drove Penney into work, where she gave them a tour of the newly renovated building. After receiving their accolades, she sent them off for the morning. It would be a relatively quiet morning with no students, the day devoted to teachers working together. Penney sat in briefly on a few department meetings and then returned to her office to meet with the cheerleading coach. Penney was actually enjoying sitting when she had a chance throughout the morning.

However, the conversation with the cheerleading coach had her sitting on pins and needles as the coach described the activities at a recent, non-school-sponsored event. A few of the student cheerleaders had engaged in some pretty risky behaviors, including drug and alcohol use, which had led to some rather raucous antics.

At this point in the conversation, Penney held up her hand. "I have to ask a few questions before you go on. First, where and when did this happen? Second, who was this initially reported to and by whom? Third, where were you when all this was happening?"

The cheerleading coach squirmed in her seat, her flaxen curls quivering on her tiny shoulders. "I am sorry to have to bring this to you, Mrs. Divan. It was an out-of-state competition over the long weekend. A couple of my girls brought the events to my attention. I had actually gone to bed for the evening, and their pounding on the door woke me up. The police were called and came pretty quickly, I was told. They were already on the scene when I got there. The girls' parents were too, picking up some of the clutter. It's just all a mess..."

"Okay. I'm going to call Jon and Sean in to hear your story. Then I will share the information with one of the school resource officers." Penney picked up her walkie-talkie and summoned the assistant principals.

The young coach's tears flooded her face. "I am so, so sorry... They all got a little high, but nothing else. Well, I mean, I heard their behaviors were a little obnoxious, and I guess they offended a couple of the other guests. I just feel so irresponsible."

Penney patted the coach's back as she signaled Jon and Sean to take seats in her office. "All right, let's have you share your story with these gentlemen."

When the coach left Penney's office, Jon was first to utter, "Oh! Ow! Where do we go from here?"

"I'll say," added Sean, looking dumbfounded.

Penney slumped in her seat as she quietly said, "Time to call one of the officers in."

The officer wasted no time explaining that the out-of-state police would have to inform the local police of the incident. Since the coach was at the scene and had witnessed the girls' demeanors, the coach would have to relay the facts to the athletic director. The usual committees would have to be set up, and the students and their families would be asked to present their own sides of the story. He cautioned that any or all of the coach's story could be denied.

The four of them discussed approaches to take for close to an hour. Then Penney called Frank. Visualizing him holding his head, Penney relayed what she knew and then outlined the strategy she, Jon, and Sean would pursue. They would meet with the students and their parents individually, assign appropriate suspensions, and set up community service projects for each student. Frank, as well, insisted upon meeting with the students involved and their parents, each family separately. He also wanted to meet with the coach, but with board members in attendance. Penney was certain that meant she would be looking for a new cheerleading coach soon.

When she hung up, Jon and Sean looked directly at her. "Mrs. D, this happened on our watch, so we would like to see this process through on our own as much as possible," Jon explained.

Sean added, "We've talked it over. We know you have to be at some of the meetings, but, Mrs. D, you're barely out of the hospital. We want to take most of this away from you."

"Fair enough, gentlemen, so long as you keep me informed." Penney was rightfully proud of her two assistant principals. At that moment, Ginger and Ken came through the door and whisked Penney away in short order. Penney really couldn't share much about her morning, but the thought *All in the realm of a principal's day* crossed her mind several times on the way home.

Lunch and a nap replenished Penney's resources. After her nap, Penney checked her e-mail to learn where the investigative process was. Jon and Sean had orchestrated the formal meetings with the athletic director, as well as the individual family meetings with Frank. Penney, Jon, Sean, and the athletic director were to meet with Frank and the school board tomorrow evening in a closed session. All was set; Penney had only to show up.

Penney pulled away from the computer pleased and thinking, *Those two men I am proud to say have been trained by me. Bravo, gentlemen!* Penney was happy when she went to bed that evening. Her world was spinning in the right direction again.

Penney allowed Ginger and Ken to shuttle her into the high school early the next morning. They dropped her off, promising to return in a couple of hours. Penney greeted each of her office staff and then moved to the hallway to take her customary place beside the school nurse. The students quickly filled the entryway, and most, seeing Penney, gave her a thumbs–up, a smile, and/or a hearty hi. There was not even a whisper of the cheerleading scandal circulating among the students. *The local code of silence is thankfully alive and in effect,* Penney couldn't help thinking. She had hoped for this to be the case, for this was not an event she wished broadcast. The first bell rang, and students and teachers were off to their classes.

Penney met with Jon, Sean, and the athletic director to go over everyone's notes for this evening's meeting with Frank and the school board. All agreed they were prepared. Moving on, Penney next met with Jon and Sean to discuss the guidance and math departments' recent interactions and the current status between the two departments. As the meeting was winding down, Jon mentioned that he had run into Angie downtown when he had dropped some things off at central office. He indicated that Angie had said she was very worried about Penney.

Penney sat upright in her chair and asked, "What might she be worried about?"

"Well, she knows you are very ill and is concerned that you are still working." Sean shot Jon a warning look.

"Now, how would she know how ill I may or may not be? Angie, like so many others, just assumes. They don't ask. Assumptions can be dangerous. I have cancer, not typhoid, and I am winning the battle right now. Cancer does not consume my days. It is a chronic illness that needs to be addressed but not given license to take over my or anyone else's life. I am a wife, a mother, a grandmother, a high school principal, a world traveler, and many, many other things, and I happen to have cancer. I am living my life to the fullest extent possible. Next time, tell her to ask me herself how I am."

"Penney, just so you know, I did tell her you were dealing with the cancer and with the job quite well."

"Thank you. Now I think I will go do an observation before I need to leave." Penney grabbed her observation folder, waved to the two men, and exited her office.

Jon and Sean looked at one another. Sean broke the silence by suggesting, "Maybe we should move on with our days too. Man, she has grit!"

"That she does! Let's get back to work."

When the foursome met that evening with Frank and the board, they were formidable. They presented the facts, outlined their strategy, and fielded questions with alacrity. After the meeting, Frank and the school board all agreed the high school was in very good hands.

By the end of the week, Penney was driving herself to work and meeting Ginger for coffee after seeing Karishma, Rita, or Cree on different days. Penney was quickly moving back into her comfort zone. She was able to get in quite a few teacher observations when she was at the high school. This made it possible for her to be highly visible to staff and students alike. All marveled at her stamina. With three observers of her at home, Penney was reminded to rest. It was a good, well-balanced couple of weeks. Seeing Ginger and Ken off on a Saturday morning, Penney was sad to see them go but was fully aware that they had to return to their own lives.

Monday she saw Dr. Tirion and experienced her first post-surgery saline injection into her tissue expander. Dr. Tirion explained she would feel a little pressure during the injection. Truth be told, the pressure was actually pretty intense. Penney knew she would be glad when this procedure was complete. Since it had to be repeated until the expander was slightly larger than the other breast, it was going to take a few more injections to be complete. It was all part of the process, so Penney was prepared to keep moving on, pressure and all.

Back at work, she completed her second quarter observations and monitored the cheerleading incident investigation, including meeting with a couple of the parents hoping for clemency for their daughters. She listened but did not alter the sanctions originally determined. Her scars were healing, her body was resting, and her mind and heart were open to being fair and firm. The choices one makes in life can often have consequences we are not fully anticipating. How well Penney knew this axiom to be true.

Thursday evening's high school music concert put both her and Jack in the holiday spirit. Friday, she had a follow-up appointment with Dr. Tirion, who appeared very pleased to announce that Penney was healing extremely well. He was looking forward to seeing Penney in January for her next tissue expansion injection. *Oh boy! Me too!* thought Penney. When Jack and Penney boarded the plane on Saturday for their annual trip to Mexico, they were ready to really relax and enjoy one another.

The trip to Mexico was not a vacation so much anymore as it was a return to their second home. They knew the people, the places, and the specialness of the area. Whales breached the ocean waters just steps away from their condo. The whale, long a totem animal for Penney, represented creative expression and spiritual expansion for her. She did indeed believe she was growing in many arenas. Penney literally gulped in the clean desert air while watching the mighty animals frolic in the water. The sheer graceful power of the whales always took her breath away. Many joined her along the coastline to take in the whales' primal majesty. She had much to contemplate in this most idyllic of settings. Jack came up behind her and encircled her in his arms.

"Want to catch some sun before we walk into town for lunch?"

"Sure. Give me about ten minutes, and I'll be ready to go." Penney had found a swimsuit the day before when they were walking around after moving into their condo and looking for a place to eat. She saw it in the window, walked into the store, tried it on, and bought it on the spot. She now pulled up the top, making sure the area where her pecs had been was not readily noticeable. The red and white polka dots carried the eye away from her underarm areas. For her head, she also found a bandana that coordinated with the swimsuit perfectly. Taking stock one last time in the mirror, Penney took a deep breath. *Well, here goes nothing. I can do this!*

Together she and Jack found a discreet corner where she could luxuriate in the sun's rays and he could read in the shade. When Penney got up to stretch and then arrange herself to sun on the opposite side, she noticed one woman nearby who was staring pretty intently at her. Penney just figured it was her swimsuit. It was pretty cute, after all.

Thirty minutes was all the time Penney needed in the sun. She and Jack decided to pack up and prepare themselves to walk into town. As Penney stood, the same woman who had been staring was still staring and said out loud, "Oh, now I understand." Looking directly at Penney now that their eyes met, the woman said, "That is a very cute swimsuit." There was no mistaking that her eyes were riveted on Penney's missing pec areas.

"Thanks!" answered Penney as she tugged at her top and tied her straps behind her neck. *This too shall pass. But damn that nubbin!* From then on, Penney made sure the area was less likely to draw attention as she continued to catch a few healthy rays of the sun every day. Life went on.

Jack made Penney lie down every afternoon. She knew it was necessary, so she gave in to a power nap each day. When not sleeping, Penney read. She also took advantage of watercolor lessons that another guest was offering. By the end of the two weeks, Penney's watercolors were showing promise. She began to see the desert come to life on her paper—the colors, the textures, and its own life. Penney had to admit the painting was yet another way to relax and get in some serious life reflection.

As always, Penney and Jack discovered a few new restaurants, one of which really stood out among the rest. When the taxi picked them up, they assumed they would be dropped off at yet another resort. However, when they entered a tunnel lit up by torches, they knew the evening promised to be something extra-special. Their taxi was met by a guide, who took them along a bougainvillea-strewn path leading them to an outdoor restaurant set into the side of a mountain. Ocean waves crashed on the rocks below them while the hypnotic rhythms of a twelve-stringed guitar filled the air. The food was equally exquisite, making the evening truly magical.

As was now his custom, Jack gazed across the table at Penney. "Penney, you know you amaze us all!"

"Jack, it's not amazing. It's survival. I need more time because I have a whole lot more I want to do and see. It's that simple." Penney winked at Jack.

Jack shook his head and then asked, "Mind if I keep coming along for the ride?"

"Oh, Jack! Of course not! What are best friends for?" Her words were spontaneous, and she realized how truly lucky she was.

"I like having you as a friend, Penney." Jack raised his glass, and Penney raised hers.

"Now, Jack, what shall we do tomorrow?" The waves were now gently breaking on the rocks below them. The moon took it all in.

They decided to ride the local bus, always an adventure, over to a neighboring town the next day. It would be Christmas Day, and they could feel a new bauble coming Penney's way.

The bus ride had the usual surfers exiting onto the sand, the water on the distant horizon. There were stops at resorts along the way where service staff got off to begin a shift, and others got on, as their shifts had ended. There were young families dressed to the nines on their way to visit family members for a Christmas Day celebration. There were also other tourists pulling the cord to signal a stop along the way to exit to an American restaurant. Not so for Penney and Jack! When they reached their destination, they sought out a restaurant offering dishes native to the region. After a leisurely lunch beginning with *el queso fundido a la Mexicana* followed by *el chile en nogada* for Penney and *la conchinita pibil* for Jack, and ending with a shared *pastel de tres leches,* Jack aided Penney in finding the perfect pair of amber earrings. The ancient fossilized stones glimmered with flecks of molasses-colored debris floating through the burnished hues of a Baja sunset. The earrings were a lovely reminder of the raw beauty of the area.

It was a good day, as were all the days on the Baja. The crowning jewel was usually New Year's Eve, and this year was no exception. Jack dressed in his tuxedo, looking sharp and suave. Penney called him her caballero. Penney wore a form-fitting little black dress emphasizing all the curves she thought she had lost but now had to admit she had rediscovered when fully clothed. It had been a while since Penney had done a body inventory, and good gracious, what a figure she appeared to now have! It was almost embarrassing, for she was over sixty, but the mirror caught Penney grinning from ear to ear. She would bask in her own beauty tonight.

Their table sat on the beach and very near the dance floor. The moon illuminated the party area. Pinks, purples, fuchsias, and teals were spun through the table settings and the overhead decorations. As the evening progressed, balloons of similar shades appeared during the line dances and could be seen bouncing among the dancers. At midnight, Penney and Jack toasted one another with champagne, ate their twelve grapes for luck, and reveled in one another's reflection of the other. Fireworks lit up the moonshine-laden sky, and the elegant partiers cast their eyes upward to see vast explosions of red, white, and green interspersed with showers of gold. The joyful festivities continued long into the night. For Penney and Jack, the new year began at the end of the dancing with plates of *huevos rancheros* and steaming mugs of coffee. They clinked their coffee mugs and wished for peace, joy, and vibrant health in the new year.

XI

The first couple of days back at work were busy. Penney was tempted to put in a little more time but knew she would see Dr. Tirion on Wednesday, so she was hoping he would make full days at work official. Taking advantage of being well rested, Penney put her half-time hours to good use. In the mornings, she met with department chairs to go over budget items and issues for preparing the next school year's budget, and she met with individual teachers to review her classroom observations. When she returned in the afternoons, she met with the school board president one day to go over her new year's wish list for the high school, and with Frank on another day to talk about personnel and curricular issues. She happened to be at the high school later on Tuesday afternoon and was able to watch the wrestling team practice, as well as see the opening plays for the junior varsity basketball game in the beautiful new gym. These student activities, as always, did her heart good.

There was more mind-bending pressure when additional saline was added to her tissue expander on Wednesday. Dr. Tirion did concede that she could return to working eight-hour days, but no more. *Yay!* He continued to be impressed with her recovery.

When Penney saw Karishma on Thursday after work, there was much to discuss—actually, more than Penney had been anticipating. First off, Karishma was concerned about Penney's new hours.

"When Dr. Tirion said you could work a full eight-hour day, I hope that doesn't quickly turn into your old twelve- to fourteen-hour day. After all, it has not been even a full two months since your surgery." Karishma's deep, searing gaze was meant to drive prickles of doubt and due consideration through Penney's being.

Penney visibly shook off the chill that suddenly came over her. "No. No. I understand. I am certain you and many others will hold me to following Dr. Tirion's instructions." Penney smiled tentatively.

Karishma held Penney's gaze for several more moments while she explored her own intuitive introspection. Karishma then took a long, lingering breath and observed, "I sense your physical health is slowly returning, but I still feel your spiritual heart you are keeping at bay. What are your thoughts?"

Before she responded, Penney collected her thoughts as she watched the clock above Karishma's head tick away the minutes. "I know that I have a long path ahead of me. I have to rebuild my physical strength and my mental stamina, and, yes, I have to reconcile some issues that worry my heart. Many expect me to be strong, and I am trying for all of us. I sometimes fear, though, that others look to me to be a beacon that they can follow or seek out. My light is there, I know, but I find myself chasing my own light sometimes, trying to catch it for me. This chase can be exhausting and occasionally downright threatening. It makes me feel very alone at times." Penney's tears fell intermittently at first and then fluttered down her cheeks like the petals on a diminished, fading flower.

Karishma came over and held Penney for a long, long time. The space around them slowly took on a warm glow. Penney had shed her fears, and Karishma could now treat Penney as she needed to be treated. There was much Penney physically had exhibited and emotionally had revealed. Their sessions would focus on multiple meridians including not only the heart, but also the liver, kidney, bladder, stomach, and lungs. Karishma would help Penney grow strong for herself and for all those others she felt bound to serve. Understanding now that these were the doors blocking Penney's reemergence, Karishma would open the pathways to make Penney free, free of the boundaries others had placed in her path. When the two of them had begun Penney's treatment, Penney's pulses were weak and ragged. When Penney's treatment was complete, her pulses were strong. Penney left Karishma that day with a firm resolve to give herself adequate time to heal.

When Penney saw Cree, Penney's aura was so strong that Cree found herself enmeshed in a golden cloak of sunshine. The session made them both stronger. At the beginning of the following week, Penney went to visit Rita. There, her guided meditation journey took her once again to the door, but this time it opened enough to reveal a light-filled forest. Nell was the next person she visited. Penney's request for renewed strength began with light, free weights—one-pound, shocking-pink, hand-held weights—which would lead to new avenues of physical endurance. Penney was on her way!

At work it was evident to all that her fire and drive were quickly rising to full gear. Penney had spoken to Frank several times about increasing the educational options for all of her students. When she met with the school board president, Penney's enthusiasm for this quest was immediately reciprocated. At a subsequent board meeting, Penney had the backing of the entire school board. She now headed a committee which oversaw subcommittees specifically looking at increasing Advanced Placement course offerings, expanding vocational/technical programming, and creating a mentor project for the academically challenged. Penney included students on each of the subcommittees. Their participation was tentative in the beginning, but they became fully engaged with the mission and had much to offer, making Penney duly proud.

Penney worked alongside Jon and Sean to continue to tweak their discipline approach, allowing staff and students to work out collective consequences themselves before turning to administration to mediate their differences. This had immediate, positive effects in two arenas. There were fewer disciplinary referrals, and the overall school climate became even more friendly and interactive. The real plus for Penney, Jon, and Sean was that they had more time to look at yet more innovations to help the total school.

Penney still struggled with issues related to her treatment prior to her surgery, notably her skin, her nails, and her energy. These she addressed with facials, whole-body scrubs, and luxurious manicures and pedicures, as well as weekly appointments with Karishma, Cree, Rita, and Nell. When she met with Dr. Saks and Dr. Tirion in early March, she was not only looking healthy but was pronounced healthy enough to begin thinking about swapping her tissue expander for a breast implant in May.

In stunned amazement sometimes, Jack watched Penney's rise from the Penney he had thought he might lose in the surgical recovery room to the Penney emerging from her morning workout flushed with health and ready to take on whatever her days brought her. Watching television one evening, they both sat transfixed viewing Machu Picchu on the travel channel.

"That is a place I have often dreamed about since I was a little girl," said Penney cryptically.

Jack looked at Penney out of the corner of his eye. "We should go there," he mused.

Penney turned to look directly at Jack. "Don't make promises you can't keep."

Jack now returned her stare. "No, seriously, let's go! I'll give Ginger a call and see what strings she can pull. I think it might be good to go before your next surgery. No sense in delaying your dream any longer." Jack grinned mischievously.

Penney jumped up, slid on to Jack's lap, and gave him a whopping big bear hug.

The planning for this upcoming trip was sheer fun. They would fly to Lima and spend the night before moving on to Cusco and the Sacred Valley. Machu Picchu would await them near the end of their journey. In the planning, Penney specifically requested that she get to visit with a shaman. Ginger called at one point to say that that was no longer allowed nor done on these types of excursions. To this, Penney pointed out that considering what this venture was going to cost, she would indeed be expecting a session with a shaman. It was back to the drawing board for Ginger and back to anticipating a dream come true for Penney.

When not immersed in travel planning, Penney interviewed and hired a new cheerleading coach, chaired committee meetings, mediated between the guidance and math departments, and took her usual keen, hands-on interest in managing the high school and its many diverse activities, as well as maintaining her integrative care program. Karishma, Cree, and Rita had all been to Machu Picchu, and they were anxious for Penney to experience its healing energies.

April arrived and Lima loomed on the horizon. It would be the end of the rainy season in Peru. Penney and Jack packed layers of clothing. Still having an adverse reaction to damp cold, Penney wanted to be prepared to stave off the chill. Lima proved to be warmer than expected when they arrived late in the evening. A warm breeze made the walk to the airport hotel a delightful transition from the long plane ride.

Early the next morning, Penney and Jack rose to catch the first peeks of sunshine escorting them along their flight to Cusco. There they were met by a limo driver, who shepherded them to a magnificent structure straight out of an earlier period of time. The luxurious hotel emerged among the streets of Cusco, quietly elegant. Spanish and Incan ghosts silently beckoned to the travelers entering this world. At the reception desk, Penney and Jack were given their first cups of coca tea to ease altitude sickness. They hoped this mildly bitter green tea would do its trick high in these cloud forests of the Andes.

Cusco turned out to be an unexpected treasure rich with Spanish and Incan influences. It was here at the cathedral where they learned from their guide that it was the church, and not the military, who seduced the Incas in order to seize the riches of the Incan empire. The ruins littered the city streets, each with their tale of how the Spanish had intertwined themselves into the local cultural structure. That structure was well represented among characters participating in a local festival one evening. At this gathering there were historical reenactments, exotically costumed dancers, rich foods, and plenty of locals for Penney and Jack to mingle with as they marveled at the mysteries being unlocked throughout the night. A world of magic and mysticism was opening up for them.

Penney and Jack next wended their way through the Sacred Valley. Here they found series after series of steep agricultural terraces and hilltop fortresses. Trails led over and through the terraces, tunnels, temples, tombs, and ceremonial structures. According to their guide, all had been engineered by the Incas for farming, worshipping, and bathing.

Penney and Jack learned the food was pretty good too. They dined on creative Andean dishes such as passion fruit–glazed trout, alpaca steak in a red wine reduction with quinotta and wild mint lemonade, and topped off with a rainforest chocolate Brazil nut torte. Large clay ovens dotted the valley, always yielding fluffy empanadas. Penney and Jack could not bring themselves to try the guinea pigs, locally called *cuy,* a common protein in the area. As they watched the guinea pigs scurry around their small pens designed to resemble castles, Penney and Jack just knew they could not have these particular unsuspecting creatures make their way onto their plates. Visions of their own childhood pets danced before their eyes. In every other instance, however, Penney and Jack thoroughly enjoyed the Novoandino cuisine.

The ruins continued to amaze them, as did their very knowledgeable guide, whose bounty of historical information was endless. They walked among beauty every day and were treated to decadent delights. One day at the foot of part of the Inca Trail, they dined on a picnic lunch, complete with white tablecloth and white wine. Dining another day at a hacienda, they ate Inca delicacies, including heart of beef brochettes paired with grilled corn and fried yucca, all surprisingly delighting their palates. Here at the hacienda, they also enjoyed a show of Peru's Paso horses doing an intricate ballet of sorts with exquisitely attired female dancers. It was at the hacienda where Penney was visited by the shaman.

All there—Jack, the chef, the waiters, the dancers, and the horses with their riders—fell back respectfully as the shaman spread out his instruments and silently invoked the spirit to walk with him and the woman he had been brought to heal. Penney and Jack's guide provided translation and interpretation from the side. The shaman explained through chant and song that he sensed an illness needed to be mended by doing some work with Penney's soul. This would help restore her physical body's balance. As balance in her life grew, there would be less and less need for her to worry about her illness returning.

Jack stole several looks toward Penney as she sat mesmerized by this little man who had never met her until today and yet seemed to know her wildest dreams and most worrisome fears. *It's eerie and strange, but could there be something to this? Hmmm...* Penney's sharing of her previous experiences with spirituality actually made her time with this shaman more than just another curiosity for Jack.

The shaman drummed and chanted and journeyed with Penney's soul. Penney's eyes were closed as she too moved along in this journey. The shaman passed the rattle around her a couple of times and ended by holding the hawk feathers over her head. One could hear the breeze pass as a hawk was seen flying over the group. For a long time, all was silent. When Penney did look up, the shaman held her gaze for a few moments. His smoky, dark eyes still looked into her soul. She let a smile drift to her mouth. The shaman smiled back at her and presented her with a cluster of coca leaves, and then he vanished. The others continued to remain respectfully still while Penney continued to reflect on the words of the shaman. Again, the message was clear. She would continue to grow strong for herself first, and then for others. Penney turned to Jack and smiled that smile he loved so well. Jack winked and said, "Now, that was something!" The group broke up later that afternoon with each person quietly reflective as they went their separate ways.

The next day, Penney and Jack took the train to Aguas Calientes, checked into their hotel, and met their guide to catch the bus to Machu Picchu. After they checked in at the desk, their guide escorted them to the entrance. Rounding the corner, Penney's dream rushed at her senses. The vistas across the ancient city offered ghostly whispers, and the onslaught of energy from every direction brought Penney to her knees as the beams bombarded her, piercing every fiber in her being. Jack waved the guide away, saying only, "She has been waiting for this her whole life. Let's let her take it in her way."

The vastness of the ruins was inspiring and unexpected. The city spilled over the mountainsides. Laced by long wisps of clouds, tiers and tiers of homes vacant of household items were eerily filled with the whispers of ancestors claiming the land that visitors now walked upon. Temples grew out of the order designating where the various socioeconomic groups had resided. Caves pockmarked the cliff walls where the bones of the ancestors could be found. In every direction, this ancient city spread before Penney as a testimony to the power of persistence. When their guide offered to lead Penney across the Inca Bridge, Penney scaled the mountain with ease and sprightly negotiated the narrow bridge. She could not help but feel she had lived here once in an earlier life and walked the bridge before. Penney looked about her and could not shake the notion that she was immersed in a dream, the clouds her stepping stones, the ancestors' whispers on the breeze her daily creed, and the orderliness of this ancient civilization her own validation for hope. As the clouds rose and slowly cleared, the doors Penney had found closed so often before now opened onto this wonderland of faith and quiet splendor. Penney could only drink in the life-giving blood of hope and taste the essence of the beauty surrounding her.

Jack came up behind her, putting his hands on her shoulders. "Penney, this will be in my dreams from now on too. This is truly awesome!"

The euphoria from this trip stayed with Penney through her implant surgery and throughout those final months and days of the school year. When she came to the podium at graduation this year, Penney appeared taller than life itself to all who heard her deliver her final address to the class of 2009.

The breeze was gentle but discernible. Hardly a cloud was in the sky, a sky not unlike the sky which had held her gaze at Machu

Picchu very recently. Penney began to speak from the depths of her soul after her formal greetings to all those present:

"Dr. Ferrari, members of the school board, parents, relatives, friends, members of the community, and you the members of the class of 2009, a warm good evening to you all!

"I would like this evening to share some reflections upon my journey of the last few years, for all of you have helped me persevere along the way.

"'Courage,' it has been said, 'is not the towering oak that sees storms come and go'; but rather, 'it is the fragile blossom that opens in the snow.'

"I do not consider myself necessarily a courageous person, but I do know that there were decisions I had to make very early on in my journey that were very much like the petals of a flower opening up each day, one by one, slow, steady, and sure, in spite of the snows falling all around me.

"And the first one had to do with a song. While I had lost this memory for a time, it recently came rushing back at me. My wise husband took me in his arms that first day when I learned of my diagnosis and said, 'Remember our song.' Yes, we who have extended life experience also have our songs. I listened to that song for days and came to one very clear and sound conclusion."

Emanating from a lone saxophone played near the stage, the silky, sinuous strains of a ballad from years long past coiled around the warm air of the evening and filled the stadium. Penney continued.

"We had promised to spend all of our lives together, and we had agreed to make one another's wishes come true. I realized there was much ahead of us.

"My first choice then was soon very clear. My dreams would be shared with my best friend, my soul mate, and the love of my life. And my vision and my days would be shared with all of you.

"Whether they were good, bad, or ugly, you have shared those days with me. As you flashed your smiles in the hallway, brought home victories, sometimes even fought your own demons; I have watched you make choices, and I have watched many of you grow in the knowledge of having to live with the consequences of your decision making, good or bad.

"For a long while, I found it hard to fall asleep because I worried that I would not wake. There have been many who fostered that fear for me as they pondered a diagnosis they know little about. Then one morning, I woke up and realized I myself had come to know a great deal about my diagnosis and a great deal about what I would like to accomplish, and ultimately I discovered hope. At that moment, I made another choice and a decision—that I would live each day as a gift given to me to share. Further, I would start quietly battling—well, maybe not so quietly always, but battling—the naysayers and begin to share a positive message of hope.

"The Scot, Samuel Smiles, has said, 'Hope is the companion of power and the mother of success: for who so hopes strongly has within him the gift of miracles.'

"Miracles are, after all, impossible things that happen anyway. You enter a world fraught with cynics and negative thinkers. Yes, life will sometimes be tough. I do indeed respect the challenges you will face. But persevere and be diligent in following through with your convictions. The challenges that you will face will shape the choices that you make. Those choices will shape your destiny and tender the mercy of miracles.

"My own convictions have always been pretty clear, and I do believe in the dream and the promise of the future. I no longer believe physical and mental challenges can compromise my will to bring clarity and well-being to my body, mind, and spirit. I have had to be creative. Challenge is, after all, an opportunity. If anything, my journey is the ultimate opportunity to be creative and to take action.

"So I would ask each of you to go into the world with the knowledge that you will succeed and that you will draw upon your own personal reserves of courage, bravery, hope, and endurance to be your best, to bring out the creativity in others, and to meet your own personal challenges with care for others and with conviction to move toward success.

"May you bring positive energy to the lives of others! Thank you all!"

Following the tossing of the caps, Penney turned and walked cheerily off the stage. As she made her way across the field this year, students, parents, staff members, community members, and complete strangers came up to her to compliment her on her speech and on the brave example she set for all of them. Many gave her hugs. Her step became lighter as she approached her car. Then she stopped.

There was Jack leaning against her car, waiting for her with open arms. *Jack is never here for graduation,* she thought as she ran to him.

"Just thought I would come and see what all the hoopla is about every year. Quite a speech, Penney. I had forgotten about our song for a while. All those hugs from the graduates as you pass out diplomas… I guess I didn't realize I had so much competition. Remember one thing, though, Penney. Nobody loves you like I do. That's just what I am going to be doing too, loving you." Jack squeezed her tight.

Penney looked up and saw the stars reflected in Jack's eyes. She felt the energy pulsing all around her. They swayed and hummed to their song together and just kept hugging. The few lingering clouds had cleared, and the moon encapsulated the two of them in its glow.